Penguin Books
The White Cottage Mystery

Margery Allingham took to writing naturally; in her family no other occupation was considered natural or indeed sane. Educated at the Perse School and Regent Street Polytechnic, she wrote her first novel while still in her teens. She began to leave a lasting mark on modern fiction in 1928 when, at the age of twenty-three, she wrote the first of her Albert Campion detective novels. Her early books, such as *The Crime at Black Dudley*, *Mystery Mile* and *Look to the Lady*, had to be written in spare time hard won from her film work. At that time her books were beloved by the few advanced spirits who enjoyed her gay and distinctive approach to the problems and pleasures of post-war youth. Since then her gentle detective and his strong-arm colleagues have become known and loved by readers of all ages all over the world. She also acquired a reputation as a more serious writer. In an *Observer* review of *The Fashion in Shrouds* Torquemada remarked that 'to Albert Campion has fallen the honour of being the first detective to feature in a story which is also by any standard a distinguished novel'. Her novels cover a broad field. They vary in treatment from the grave to the frankly satirical, yet each example contrives to conform to the basic rules of the good detective tale.

Margery Allingham was married to Philip Youngman Carter and lived for many years on the edge of the Essex Marshes. She died in 1966.

Margery Allingham

The White Cottage Mystery

Penguin Books

Penguin Books Ltd, Harmondsworth, Middlesex, England
Penguin Books, 625 Madison Avenue, New York, New York 10022, U.S.A.
Penguin Books Australia Ltd, Ringwood, Victoria, Australia
Penguin Books Canada Ltd, 2801 John Street, Markham, Ontario, Canada L3R 1B4
Penguin Books (N.Z.) Ltd, 182–190 Wairau Road, Auckland 10, New Zealand

First published in book form 1928
This edition first published by Chatto & Windus 1975
Published in Penguin Books 1978
Reprinted 1983

Made and printed in Great Britain by
Richard Clay (The Chaucer Press) Ltd,
Bungay, Suffolk
Set in Monotype Times

Preface

Many Margery Allingham fans have asked where they can obtain a copy of *The White Cottage Mystery*. This was the author's first detective story and was published in 1928, having previously appeared as a newspaper serial in the *Daily Express*.

In the lists of her published works this title is seldom included. The reason for this omission is that she had written the story specifically as a serial, with no thought of subsequent book publication, whereas her later Campion tales, those which brought her fame, were conceived in the first place with hard covers in mind.

To enable the casual newspaper reader to keep pace with the story of *The White Cottage Mystery* easily, she had employed the time-honoured device of re-emphasizing in each instalment certain vital elements of the plot. Much later, whenever the question of re-issue in book form arose, Margery felt that to let the tale appear as it stood, without editing, could only cause disappointment to her new circle of regular readers, and, as she never had the time to carry out the revision, she pushed aside all requests for re-publication.

Well aware of the pleasure her stories have given and continue to give to so many, and since the necessary editing merely involved cutting out superfluous repetitions, I have taken it upon myself to attempt this; the result is, I believe, what Margery intended. I hope that her many friends will not only enjoy this detective tale but will want to add the book to their collections.

Tolleshunt D'Arcy   *Joyce Allingham*
May 1974

1   The Girl with the Blister on Her Heel

It was a little after four o'clock in the evening when Jerry Challoner swung his sports car smartly round the bend in the Kentish road and slid quietly through the village street.

At the moment he was well contented with life. He was making good time and there was no need to hurry, since London was but thirty miles ahead. The autumn evening was sunny, and he felt as he glanced in front of him that there could be no other place in the world more peaceful.

Even the red bus which passed at the crossroads seemed to be a gentler, more domesticated creature than its wilder brethren of the London streets.

A girl alighted from the bus. As he approached, the conductor handed her out a large basket, ringing his bell immediately afterwards, so that by the time Jerry arrived she was standing there alone struggling with it.

The next moment found the car drawn up beside her and Jerry leaning over the side.

'I say,' he said. 'Can't I give you a lift?'

The girl turned round upon him.

'God bless you! It's about half a mile down this road, and I've such a blister on my heel!'

'That's fine,' he said, as a moment or two later she settled herself beside him. 'Where's the house?'

'Down here on the right – it's called White Cottage. I'll point it out to you; it's just the other side of that big grey building.'

'That's a queer place. What is it? An institution?'

'Oh no; that's a private house.'

Jerry looked at the great barrack of a place they were approaching with a certain amount of surprise.

'A private house?' he said. 'Good lord! Who lives there? – it looks like a hospital.'

'Doesn't it!' said the girl, and laughed; but she did not answer his question, and he had a fleeting impression that it had embarrassed her. They had passed the hideous building by this time, and the girl touched his arm.

'Look!' she said. 'Here we are.' She pointed towards a white house set far back from the road, surrounded by shrubbery.

Jerry drew up before the gate and helped the girl out.

'I'll bring the basket along for you, shall I?'

'Well – no, thanks awfully, if you don't mind,' she said, and she seemed curiously disconcerted.

'Oh, all right!' he said cheerfully. 'I'll leave it here, shall I? You can send someone down for it afterwards; don't carry it yourself with that heel.'

He turned to go back to the car as he spoke, conscious that she did not want him to stay a moment longer than was absolutely necessary.

'Good-bye.'

'Good-bye,' she repeated, 'and thanks.'

A storm was blowing up fast, and already a few heavy drops had begun to fall. A little way down the road therefore he pulled up again to put the hood up, and as he did so took the opportunity to have a cigarette. He found that he had no matches, however, and was about to push on again when a policeman turned the corner and came down the path towards him.

Jerry borrowed the necessary match and the two fell into conversation.

'Storm coming up,' said Jerry.

'There is, indeed,' said the policeman, who was red-headed. 'We get some wonderful weather down in these parts on account of the hills.'

The sound of footsteps on the road ahead disturbed him, and with the instinctive curiosity of the countryside he glanced up as a man strode past them. He was considerably over the general height, pale with a lank unshaven chin. He was bare-headed and his dry black hair was swept back from his face by the driving wind.

He walked fast and vanished round the corner without once glancing to the right or left.

Jerry looked after him, struck by the same vague expression of apprehension in the man's face that he fancied he had noticed in the girl's. From round the bend behind them came the click of a latch, and he was reminded of the gate leading down to the White Cottage where he had left the girl. The stranger must have entered it.

He turned to the constable.

'I think I'll push on,' he said.

The policeman opened his mouth to reply, but he was interrupted by the sudden report of a shot-gun somewhere to the right of where they stood. He paused and frowned.

'It's getting dark for shooting,' he said. 'Specially so near the road. These fellers round here don't realize that this road ain't the lonely lane it used to be. I've had several complaints lately of folk being scared to come along here in the evening, afraid they should be took for a rabbit or summat. If you'll excuse me, sir, I'll go and see if I can set eyes on that chap.'

Jerry climbed back into the car, and was just about to press the starter when a cry behind made him turn and peer through the window.

A girl was flying down the road towards him, her face white and terrified. She was screaming hysterically at the top of her voice:

'Police! Police! Police! Murder!'

The red-headed policeman ran towards her, and Jerry climbed out of his car once more and hurried after him.

As he came up the girl pointed behind her.

'It's the White Cottage,' she said breathlessly. ''E's in there all covered a blood.' On the last word she reeled forward, and Jerry was just in time to catch her as she collapsed.

He was the first to speak.

'Do you know her?'

The policeman nodded.

'She's the parlourmaid at the White Cottage,' he said. 'We'd best go along there. Can you manage her feet, sir, if I take her shoulders?'

The storm was coming nearer at every moment, and the heavy clouds overhead shed an unnatural darkness over the scene. The laurel bushes round the White Cottage were rustling together in the fidgety wind that precedes a downpour.

Jerry and the constable carried the fainting girl through the wicket-gate and stumbled down the path with her.

As they came up to the front door it was thrown open and a grey-faced, horror-stricken girl came running out into the porch.

Jerry hardly recognized her as the same one he had set down at the gate less than ten minutes before. All the light and youth seemed to have been drawn from her face and her blue eyes were wide.

'Oh, I'm glad you've come!' she said breathlessly. 'Something horrible has happened. Come in at once.'

Jerry and the policeman set the maid down in a chair in the porch and followed the girl into the house.

They found themselves in a square hall, neat and white-painted, with four doors leading off from it. Three of these were open, showing glimpses of bright rooms within. The fourth was closed, and a group of silent horror-stricken people stood staring at it.

Jerry followed the direction of their eyes and saw a slow dark stain oozing out from beneath the door. It showed up very clearly on the pale-grey lino although it was almost twilight in the hall.

The red-headed policeman strode forward and, stepping carefully to avoid the mark, laid a hand on the door-knob.

'Don't go in!'

The words were uttered in an hysterical scream, and a woman in the group started forward impulsively. Jerry, glancing at her for the first time, saw how much she resembled his acquaintance of early in the afternoon. She was older, perhaps, and a little more frail, but the likeness was unmistakable.

The policeman removed his hand from the knob and regarded her doubtfully.

'What's up in there?' he demanded suspiciously.

'Don't go in – it's too horrible.'

The woman began to sob on the last words, and there was a general movement in the group about her as with a sudden squeaking of wheels a man in a hand-propelled invalid-chair shot forward, and Jerry and the policeman found themselves looking down into the pale, harassed face of a man aged about five-and-thirty. His head and shoulders were those of a giant; but the rest of him was attenuated and terribly crippled. He spoke hurriedly in a quiet voice that was in direct contrast to the woman's hysteria.

'You know me, constable,' he said. 'Thank God you've come. A most appalling thing has happened. Mr Crowther of the "Dene" has been shot. He is lying in there just inside the door. My wife came in through the french windows and found him . . . be careful how you go in.'

The policeman grasped the door-handle once more.

Jerry followed him into the room.

The dead man was lying on his back in a pool of blood just inside, his face uplifted and the upper part of his shirt and coat torn aside.

From his waist to his neck he had been almost blown to pieces.

Jerry turned away, his gorge rising. As he did so he saw a single-barrel shot-gun lying on the square dining-table in the centre of the room; the barrel was pointing towards the door, and he noticed that a great part of the velour tablecloth had been blown away by the shot.

The policeman hesitated no longer, but drew out his notebook; his hand trembled as he held the pencil.

Jerry turned to him and produced his card.

'Constable,' he said. 'I'm Jerry Challoner, the son of Detective Chief Inspector W. T. Challoner of the Yard.'

2 W.T.

Many people seeing W. T. Challoner for the first time made the mistake of thinking that his nickname, the 'Greyhound', was a joke. He was a fresh-faced, inoffensive-looking man with white hair, bright eyes and an engagingly fatherly manner. No one had ever inquired and the unobservant might have placed his age at sixty had they not noticed the peculiar alertness of his step and the faint indication of enormous back muscles beneath his grey jacket.

The detective stood in the morning-room at the back of the house that had been placed at his disposal and faced his colleagues in the case – the red-headed constable and the heavy-faced inspector from New Campington. Jerry, silent and attentive, stood behind his father.

'Well,' W.T. said genially, 'I think we may as well begin our preliminary inquiry now, don't you?'

'By all means.'

The inspector seemed to welcome the authority of the older man.

The detective turned to the police constable.

'Let me see,' he said. 'You have the names of everyone in the house at the time of the crime, and as many particulars as you could collect about them?'

The red-headed policeman nodded and produced his note-book.

The detective sat down at the table and spread the book out before him.

'Now,' he said with the air of one talking aloud to himself, 'whom have we? Roger William Christensen, the owner of the house. Is that the chap in the invalid-chair I saw as I came in?

Eva Grace Christensen, his wife – she found the murdered man, I understand ... Norah Phyliss Bayliss, her sister.'

Jerry pricked up his ears – so her name was Norah.

The detective went on reading.

'Joan Alice Christensen, the Christensens' baby; Estah Phillips, nurse to the child; Kathreen Goody, 17, parlourmaid; Doris James, 40, cook ... Ah! Is that everyone, constable?'

'I think so, sir.'

'Good. Now how about the murdered man – who was he?'

The policeman stepped forward and turned over the page of the notebook.

'It's all there, sir,' he said.

The detective beamed.

'Splendid! I see – Eric Crowther, of the "Dene". Where's that?'

'The big grey building next door.'

'Did he live there alone – no wife, no servants?'

'No wife, but servants. His valet is in the next room,' said the inspector, his thick voice sounding unexpectedly in the silence that followed the question. 'I had him brought over as soon as I came.'

'Very wise, Inspector,' said W.T.; 'I think we'll have him in at once, constable.'

The policeman disappeared, to return a moment or so later with an untidy man. His small eyes were pale and there was a crop of unattractive dampish yellow-grey hair about his face and chin.

He came creeping in, the policeman's hand on his shoulder as if he were already arrested, and paused before the table without looking up.

The detective sat looking at him in silence for some seconds, his bright eyes grown keen and piercing. Suddenly an exclamation escaped him: 'Clarry Gale!' he said.

The man winced and his eyes flickered as he glanced at the detective before him.

The next moment a timorous smile spread over his face.

'W.T.!' he murmured. 'What a miracle! 'Ow are you, guv'nor?'

The detective did not smile.

'What are you calling yourself now?' he inquired.

'William Lacy, sir.'

'Good! Take all this down in shorthand, Jerry, will you? ... All right, Gale, don't get alarmed; you shall have your dues. Now answer me. How long have you been in Crowther's employ?'

'Ten years.'

The words were spoken with such a world of feeling that every eye in the room was turned upon the speaker instantly.

Even the 'Greyhound' seemed surprised.

'Ten years?' he said. 'That's ever since you came out of Wormwood Scrubs isn't it? Did he know your record?'

The man who called himself William Lacy nodded.

'Yes.'

'You've been going straight for ten years, then?'

'Yes.'

'I must congratulate you, Gale.' The detective was plainly puzzled, but he questioned the man no further about himself. When next he spoke it was to talk of the dead man.

'How long has Crowther had the "Dene"?'

'About six years.'

'Has he known the Christensens all that time?'

'*And* before.'

The detective nodded understandingly.

'You would call them old friends of his, then,' he said. 'He knew them well enough to walk into this house without knocking?'

'He did that with most people 'e knew,' declared Gale. 'No one wouldn't 'ave the nerve to stop '*im* coming in anywhere, if they wanted him or if they didn't.'

The detective looked up sharply.

'What kind of a man was he?' he said. 'Was he well liked in the neighbourhood?'

With an expression of hatred made all the more horrible by

the weakness of the face it clothed, Clarry Gale drew in a long whistling breath through his discoloured teeth.

'He was a devil,' he said, and he spoke fervently and as though he had made no exaggeration.

A flicker of interest passed over the faces of the four listeners, and the detective continued:

'Do you know why he came across here today?'

'To find Mrs Christensen.'

'Do you know why he wanted her?'

'He'd been waiting for her since half past three and she didn't come.'

'Did Mrs Christensen often visit Crowther?'

'No. He'd often taken her into New Campington in his car, but she never came to the "Dene" alone, although I know he was always fidgeting her to. I took a note over to her this morning, though, and 'e told me 'e was expecting 'er this afternoon.'

'Did he seem angry when he left the "Dene?"'

''E was never angry – 'e was just laughin', curse 'im.'

'And that was the last you saw of him alive?' continued the detective.

Gale nodded.

'It was,' he said, and with something strangely like relief in his voice.

W.T. paused for a moment, then he looked up.

'Well, that will do. I'll send for you again later. Oh, by the way – just one thing. How many other servants are there over at the "Dene" beside you?'

'Only the cook,' said the man, hesitating in the doorway. 'Nice old party she is, by name of Fisher, Mrs Elsie Fisher.'

'I see. There were only you three living at the "Dene", then.'

'Yes, sir, only us three and Mr Cellini.'

The detective pricked up his ears.

'Mr Cellini?' he inquired. 'Who's he?'

'The Italian chap what lived with the guv'nor.'

'His companion?'

'Something of that sort.'

'I see. And this man is an Italian. Was he on equal footing with your master? I mean was he in the position of a friend?'

'Oh no, they weren't *friends*.'

There was the ghost of a smile on the old lag's face, and the detective glanced at him sharply.

'What do you mean by that?' he demanded.

Clarry Gale sneered.

''E 'adn't no *friends*,' he said. 'Mr Cellini felt the same towards 'im as most of us, I reckon.'

'And how was that?'

''E 'ated 'im!'

There was an almost ferocious intensity in the man's voice, and the detective sat back in his chair.

'You yourself, of course, have a pretty strong alibi, I suppose, Gale?' he said.

'Me? I been with Mrs Fisher in the kitchen ever since lunch.'

A faint smile appeared on the detective's face.

'So I imagined,' he said. 'If you hadn't your animosity towards your late employer might have been misunderstood. However – where is Mr Cellini now?'

'Over in his room, I expec'. 'E spends most of 'is time in there when 'e can get away from the guv'nor.'

'You didn't see him before you came out?'

'No, I ain't set eyes on him all the afternoon.'

'Very well; that'll do for the present; but go over to the "Dene" and ask Mr Cellini to come across as I'd like to speak to him. Oh, and Gale – don't say anything to Mrs Fisher when you're there. Just come straight back with Cellini.'

'Righto, sir.'

On the last word the man turned and disappeared from the room with as much alacrity as ever a discharged offender stepped from the dock.

As the door closed behind him, W.T. took a deep breath.

'That was curious,' he said. 'That man was one of the most incorrigible old rogues on the books fifteen years ago. We'd lost sight of him, and now he turns up here with ten years' employment behind him, a murdered master, and an alibi. I think the next person to interview is Mrs Christensen.'

The detective rose from his chair as the door opened and Mrs Christensen and the constable came in.

Jerry recognized her as the woman who had screamed to the policeman not to go to the murdered man when they were all in the hall.

Grace Christensen was very pale and there were dark hollows under her eyes. She seemed much more composed now, however, and took the chair the detective set for her with a certain dignity.

W.T. fussed round her in a way that was peculiarly his own, behaving more like an old family doctor than a detective on a murder trail.

'Now,' he said at last when he had satisfied himself that she was comfortable and entirely at her ease, 'I don't wish to distress you, Mrs Christensen, but it would be of great assistance to me if you would tell just exactly what happened this afternoon. Don't hurry or excite yourself in any way; let us have the facts.'

The woman raised her eyes to his and spoke very softly.

'I was in the garden,' she said, 'weeding round the far side of the house; my baby was with me. I noticed a storm coming up, and I gathered up my tools, preparing to go in. I had just got them all together when I heard the shot. It was so near that I knew it must be in the house, and I ran round to see what it was. The french windows in the dining-room were open, and I went in. The gun was lying on the table, and on the floor, the other side, was ... Oh, it's too terrible to think of!' She covered her face with her hands as if to block out the sight of a horror that was still before her.

W.T. leant across the table and patted her arm soothingly.

'Never mind,' he said. 'Don't think of it. Now tell me, did you know Mr Crowther well?'

The woman looked up, a faintly scared expression in her eyes.

'He was our nearest neighbour – he used to come in to see us fairly often,' she said at last.

The detective nodded understandingly.

'He used to run in and out as he liked?' he said.

She nodded eagerly.

'Yes, that was it.'

'But you didn't go to see him in the same way?'

The scared expression returned.

'No,' she said.

The detective smiled encouragingly, his face becoming more benign and fatherly at every moment.

'How was that?'

The woman paused for a while before she replied.

'Mr Crowther was a curious man, Mr Challoner,' she said at last, and hesitated.

'You and your husband were not so fond of him as he was of you, perhaps?' suggested the detective.

'Mr Crowther was not a likeable man,' she said stiffly.

There was silence for a moment or two, and then the detective leaned across the table.

'Mrs Christensen,' he said, 'believe me, I am only trying to get to the bottom of this affair to save future unpleasantness and bother. So tell me, was your husband – jealous of Mr Crowther?'

The woman hung her head, but she did not answer, and the detective continued:

'Had he any cause?'

Still she did not reply, and he went on speaking slowly.

'You had a note from Crowther this morning asking you to go across to the "Dene" this afternoon. Why didn't you keep that appointment?'

The woman stared at him, her eyes wide and horror-stricken.

'Who told – ' she began hysterically.

'Does it matter?' interrupted W.T. gently. 'Now listen, Mrs Christensen. There is no need for you to answer my questions unless you like – you are not in a court of law. But there will be an inquest, and in your own interest it would be best for you to tell all you can about this affair.'

The woman looked at him for a minute.

'I'll tell you,' she said impulsively, and continued breathlessly as if she could not speak quickly enough.

'Eric Crowther knew me before I married, and the year after

my baby was born he came to live at the "Dene", next door. Since then he has done nothing but pester me with his attentions. Naturally I did not return them. I love my husband, but I could never escape Crowther – never shake him off. I could not forbid him the house without my husband becoming suspicious, and I had no wish for that. The last month or so he has become more persistent, and I have been at my wits' end to keep my husband from guessing the truth. This morning I had a note from him demanding that I should go over there this afternoon. I took no notice of it. The rest I have already told you.'

There was silence in the room for a moment after her voice had died away, then the detective spoke.

'Excuse me, Mrs Christensen,' he said, 'but – wouldn't it have been simpler to tell your husband all about Mr Crowther's pursuit of you in the first place?'

'Oh no . . . I couldn't do that – never – never!' There was such insistence in her voice that a suspicion that she had not yet told the whole truth sprang instantly into the minds of her listeners.

The detective hesitated.

'Mrs Christensen,' he said, 'the situation is a difficult one. You suggest that your life was made a burden to you by this man. You had a note from him this morning, you ignored it; he came across to your house presumably to fetch you – you *say* you hear a shot and go in to find him dead, but what can I think?'

The woman sat up suddenly in her chair and stared at him, her eyes glazing with surprise.

'You don't think – I – ?' she whispered. 'Oh, it's too monstrous! You can't – you don't – '

'Calm yourself, my dear lady. Nothing has been said at all yet,' said W.T., his fatherly manner returning; but the woman was terrified, and she spoke wildly.

'But you can't think of such a thing!' she insisted. 'Why, my baby was with me the whole time – she can tell you I didn't leave the garden for some moments after the shot was fired. Send for her – ask her – she'll tell you.'

The old detective understood her mood too well to refuse her, and he despatched the constable for the child.

She waited until he returned, her head held high but the shadow of fear still lurking in her blue eyes.

A few minutes later the door opened and the red-headed policeman ushered in a tall gaunt woman of sixty-five or so, who bore in her arms a sturdy little pig-tailed girl in a flannel nightgown.

W.T. smiled at her.

'Bring the baby here a moment, please,' he said.

The woman looked at him fiercely, and he was conscious that her black eyes were suspicious and hostile.

He held out his arms for the child, however, and unwillingly she gave her to him.

W.T. set the little creature on his knee, where she sat solemnly staring at him with the blank impenetrable eyes of five years old.

'What's your name?' he demanded, smiling at her blandly.

'Joan Alice,' said she after some hesitation.

'A nice name,' said the detective. 'Now, Joan Alice, you were in the garden this evening with your mother, weren't you?'

The child did not reply and the nervous woman on the other side of the table leant across to her eagerly.

'Tell him, darling,' she said, striving vainly to keep the anxiety out of her tone; 'you remember being in the garden with Mummy this evening – you remember when we pulled up the weeds so that the flowers could grow – '

'Yes,' said Joan Alice, with sudden enthusiasm, 'an' I put the weeds in my pail, didn't I?'

The woman sighed with relief, and the detective continued to question the child.

'Joan Alice,' he said, 'now try to remember hard. When you were in the garden with your mamma did you hear a big bang somewhere inside the house?'

The child did not answer him, having apparently lost interest in the proceedings; she was playing with the fountain-pen sticking out of his coat pocket.

'Joan, *darling*' – the woman's voice was frantic – 'try to remember – did you hear the bang?'

'Yes,' said the child.

'And were you with your mamma in the garden then?'

'You were, weren't you, baby?' The fear in the woman's voice was terrible to hear.

The child looked up solemnly and shook her head.

'No,' she said suddenly and distinctly. 'I was by the bonfire, entying my pail – you remember, Mumma, you sent me to.'

'Where was the bonfire?'

'Oh, down the garden a long way,' said the child, her careless tones uncanny in the tension-hung room.

'You couldn't see your mamma when you heard the bang?' The detective spoke hesitantly, as if loath to continue the inquiry.

'Oh no.'

'Joan!' There was reproach, appeal and terror in the woman's voice, and the child looked at her, frightened.

The detective rose to his feet and handed the child back to the nurse, his face very grave.

'Mrs Christensen,' he began gently, 'I'm sorry but I'm afraid I must ask you – '

The remainder of his sentence was never uttered, however, for at that moment the door was flung open unceremoniously, and Clarry Gale, his ignoble face pink with excitement, appeared breathless on the threshold.

' 'E's gone!' he announced explosively.

'Gone? Who's gone?' demanded the detective.

'Cellini, of course!' The words tumbled over one another in Gale's excitement to get them out. 'Mrs Fisher said that as soon as I come over here the first time she saw him come rushin' into the house and go up to his room. 'E was up there ten minutes; then she heard him come runnin' downstairs, go out again. Lookin' out o' the kitchen windy she saw 'im get out the guvnor's car and set off down the Folkstone road as 'ard as 'e could go. I've been up to 'is room, and 'is things are gone – 'e's bolted!'

3 The Tablecloth

'Now, my boy, they'll see to that. I think I'll return to my inquiries in the next room.' W.T. replaced the telephone receiver as he spoke.

He had just 'phoned for a general call to be put out concerning the missing Cellini.

For a moment Jerry did not speak, but looked round the room and shuddered.

'Mrs Christensen – ?' began Jerry doubtfully.

'Well, yes,' said the old man. 'She's got a secret, you know – it may be important, but it may not. That's the worst of women in a case like this, Jerry. What they think is serious and worth hiding may be the most idiotic damn' silly thing in the world, and yet they'll go and run their heads straight into a noose rather than give it away.'

He paused, staring moodily in front of him. When he spoke again his tone was like some old lawyer's vexed over a moot point.

'And there's that,' he said suddenly. 'Did you ever see anything so absurd as that?'

Jerry followed the direction of his gaze and saw that he was looking at the gun still lying on the table.

'Look at it!' W.T. repeated. 'Just look at it.'

Jerry frowned. 'I don't see . . .' he began.

'No?' said W.T. in surprise. 'Look at that tablecloth – it's blown to pieces just like Crowther's chest. That gun was fired from where it is now – it wasn't raised shoulder-high, it wasn't even fired at arm's length, as an ignorant terrified woman might have held it; it was fired from the table. At least, the butt was on the table – the barrel was raised slightly . . . A man kneeling

behind the table might have done it, but then, since he had the
point of vantage with the table between him and his unarmed,
unsuspecting enemy, why should he kneel?'

Jerry nodded. 'That's true,' he said. 'There's nothing in the
room to give any clue, I suppose?'

W.T. shook his head. 'Nothing of much use, the photographs
may show something, but I'm not hopeful. No, we can't do anything more in here yet. As soon as the doctors have finished
consulting we'll have that mess removed. But now we'll return to
the questions. I want to have a chat with that nurse – there's a
flight of stairs leading down from the nursery to the lawn just
outside these french windows. Send her in to me, will you? . . .
I'll be with the others.'

As Jerry hurried off to obey him W.T. went back to the
morning-room, and resumed his seat behind the table as the
heavy-faced inspector from New Campington was saying, 'The
woman didn't do it, Mrs Christensen didn't do it.'

'Ah,' said W.T. 'You don't think so . . . Tell me why?'

'Yes,' said the inspector.

'Had she done it, her sending the child to the bonfire at the
far end of the garden would have been a deliberate act and she
would not have forgotten it. Yet when she begged you to send for
the child she had forgotten that it was not with her when she
fired the shot.'

'That's an interesting point, Inspector. It's very true.'

The inspector nodded but W.T. was interrupted by the entrance
of Jerry and Estah Phillips, the nurse.

As soon as the detective saw the woman he again experienced
the feeling that his presence was bitterly resented.

Now that he had more leisure in which to consider her he
saw that she was a personality. Tall and gaunt, she bore her years
well, and her small, sloe-black eyes glowered at him.

Her black, unshapely frock was fastened high up at her throat,
and her face, rugged and hard, showed parchment pale above it.

She followed Jerry into the room with the dignity of a captured
general, and brusquely declined the chair the detective offered
her.

'Now,' he said, smiling at her in the most affable way imaginable – 'now, Miss Phillips, I want you to do all you can to help me in this matter.'

A sharp gust of contemptuous laughter escaped the woman, and for the fraction of a second her graven face splintered into a derisive smile.

'You'll get no help from me, so don't expect it,' she said in a voice that was harsh and vibrant.

Unexpected as this reply was, W.T. was unmoved by it. He looked at the woman shrewdly.

'You come from the Essex coast, don't you?' he said. 'Colchester way?'

It was now her turn to be surprised, and her small dark eyes flickered.

'Yes,' she said at last, her tone sullen and begrudging. 'I was born at Goldhanger near there. My folks lived there for lifetimes.'

'So I thought,' said W.T. 'Do you want to know how I told?'

'No,' said she.

'*That's* how I told,' said W.T., and smiled to himself with pardonable pleasure. 'Now,' he said, suddenly assuming an almost magisterial air, 'how long have you been in Mrs Christensen's employ?'

'Ever since she was able to pay me.'

W.T. frowned. He had no patience with literal witnesses.

'What I mean is, how long have you known her?' he said severely.

'Since she was born. I was her nurse.'

'Oh, I see.' The 'Greyhound's' tone grew more sympathetic. 'And you're very fond of her.'

'As if she were my own child.' The intensity of the words was so strong that W.T. looked up. He only caught a glimpse of the fleeting expression in the black eyes, but it was enough. He realized that he had touched on the one ruling passion of her life – deep and primitive and unbelievably strong, the mother instinct of a childless woman centred upon one creature only.

'I see,' he said quietly. 'You must do your best to help me to help her now, then.'

'Help her!' the woman burst out contemptuously. 'All you've done since you set foot in this house is to drive the poor girl nearly out of her mind – as if she hadn't enough to worry her before all this shooting set-out.'

W.T. pricked up his ears.

'*Before* the shooting?' he inquired.

The old woman paused and looked at him suspiciously.

'How much has she told you?' she demanded.

'About Mr Crowther? Everything,' said W.T. swiftly. 'Why should she hide it?'

The woman's expression did not change. The suspicion still shone in her eyes.

'No,' she said at last, 'that's true enough. He was always hanging round her. It nigh drove her off her head. He was a devil, that man.'

'No one seems to have liked him, certainly,' said W.T.

'No one had any cause,' said the old woman. 'There's no one in this house nor in his own that isn't glad to hear of his death – no one.'

'Isn't that a little sweeping, Miss Phillips?' said W.T. mildly. 'You, for instance – why should you be glad of his death?'

'Why? Wasn't he making her life a hell on earth?' said the old creature, allowing her sullen temper to flare. 'I was glad of his death. It's what I've been praying for upon my knees every night of my life for the past five years. I *am* glad of his death.'

'Think what you're saying,' protested W.T. 'The man has just been murdered. You can't go about saying things like this. What can you expect me to think?'

'It isn't anything to me what you think,' said the old woman stubbornly. 'I'm telling the truth, and the Lord in His mercy takes care of the innocent. Had I had the opportunity I won't say I wouldn't have done it.'

W.T. sat back in his chair and passed his hand over his forehead.

'I can only repeat that you're behaving very unwisely, Miss

Phillips,' he said stiffly. 'How long ago was it that Mr Crowther came to the "Dene"?'

The old woman shrugged her shoulders.

'I don't know – maybe four years, maybe five.'

'Can't you remember exactly?' W.T. insisted gently. 'Fix it by some other event in your mind.'

The woman shot a shrewd, suspicious glance at him.

'It was just over six years ago,' she said at last.

'How do you know?'

'By Jo-an's age,' she said, splitting the name with a faint trace of a country accent. 'He came just over a year afore she was born.'

'Before?' W.T. raised his eyebrows on the word. 'I thought Mrs Christensen said a year *after*.'

The old woman's eyelids flickered for an instant, but she answered stolidly, 'No, it was before. She forgot, I reckon.'

'Tell me,' said W.T. 'When Mr Crowther first came to the "Dene", were he and Mrs Christensen more – er – friendly than they were – yesterday, for instance?'

The old woman looked him squarely in the eyes.

'I know what you're thinking,' she said, 'but you're wrong. Him that's dead wasn't *that* sort of a man – he had great sins to his credit, but that wasn't one of them.'

'I see,' said W.T. 'Thank you. There's just one more thing – it's a little point, but I want everything quite clear . . . that sporting-gun in the next room, it belonged to the house, I suppose – was it always kept loaded? Who used it as a rule?'

The old woman looked at him curiously.

'He did,' she said. 'It was his gun.'

'He?' W.T. looked mystified.

The old woman regarded him stolidly. 'Him that's dead,' she said at last.

'The dead man's own gun?' exclaimed the detective, surprised out of his usual calm. 'Who brought it over? Was it in the house before today?'

The gaunt old creature hesitated, and her beady black eyes surveyed him doubtfully.

'I'm not sure if I ought to tell you,' she said at last.

W.T. leant forward across the table. 'Be sure you ought,' he said. 'I haven't come here as an enemy, Miss Phillips. I'm only doing the best I can to find out the guilty so that the innocent may be spared distress.'

The old woman looked at him gravely.

'I believe you,' she said. 'Maybe I'll tell you all I know about the gun.' She paused, and W.T. signalled to Jerry to take down what she said.

'Well,' he said at last, 'I'm listening . . .'

The old woman took a deep breath.

'Maybe you know there's a balcony outside the nursery, just above the french windows in the dining-room,' she began. 'I sit out there sometimes of an afternoon. Two days ago I was there sewing. About four o'clock it was, and I saw him that's dead coming across the lawn with the gun under his arm like as if he'd just come in from the woods. He didn't see me, though,' she went on, smiling sourly to herself; 'his mind was on the dining-room, and he passed right under me without knowing. Mr Roger was in the room,' she went on. 'Mr Christensen that is – I always call him Mr Roger – and I heard him that's dead speak to him. "Hallo, you," he said, and added on a word I'm not repeatin' to you or anyone – suggesting that *she* was unfaithful to him, as it did.' She paused.

'Go on. What did Mr Roger say?'

Old Estah hesitated.

'I'm only telling you because I believe you're acting for the good,' she said at last. 'I haven't told a word of this to another soul.'

'That's right,' said the detective encouragingly. 'You can trust us.'

'Mr Roger, he turned on him,' the old woman continued. 'Told him he ought to be ashamed of himself. Then him that's dead began to laugh – a terrible laugh he had – there's only one word for it, and that's gloating – gloating – as if he was enjoying himself. Then he said – and I heard him upon my balcony as plainly as if I'd been in there with him – "You hate me, don't you, Christensen? And you're afraid of me too, aren't you?"'

Silence had fallen upon the room as the old woman spoke, and her harsh voice sounded dramatic in the stillness.

'Mr Roger didn't reply to that,' she went on. 'And then him that's dead fell a-laughing and cursing again. "You coward!" he said, and put a word in that I'm leaving out. "If you had any spirit in you at all you'd kill me; but you daren't – you're afraid. Kill me, Christensen – I deserve it from you ... Kill me, you snivelling funk."'

She paused suddenly and instinctively lowered her voice.

'He went on taunting him, and then I heard him say quite sudden and distinctly, "Here's my gun – it's loaded. One shot of that would finish me. Take it, Christensen. Take it and fire at me. You're afraid. I know you'd never dare to shoot – but you'd like to. God! How you'd like to, Christensen! You'd have her all to yourself then. You won't take the gun? I knew you wouldn't – but I'll leave it here in the corner – it's loaded, so any time, remember – any time, you little coward – it'll always be there." And then he came out on to the lawn again, and I could see him laughing to hisself as he went off down the path.'

As her voice died away Estah looked at them anxiously.

'That's how the gun came there,' she said. 'I hope I ha'n't done wrong to tell you.'

'You've done the wisest thing you could do,' said W.T. gently. 'The truth always leaks out eventually, you know, and the earlier the better. Where were you when the shot was fired this afternoon – in the nursery?'

'No, I was in the spare room looking over the linen – go up and see it all pulled out, if you want to. Kathreen was helping me most of the time, but she'd gone down to see about tea when I heard the shot.'

'Long before?'

'About five minutes, roughly.'

'Is the spare room far from the nursery?'

'It's over this room – some way away.'

W.T. nodded.

'Thank you,' he said. 'That is all. You might ask Mr Christensen to step in here for a moment, will you? Thank you.'

As the door closed behind her Jerry smiled. 'There goes an innocent old woman, anyway,' he said.

'There goes a clever old woman,' said W.T.

Jerry looked at him in astonishment.

'Do you mean to say you don't believe her?'

W.T. shook his head.

'On the contrary, I do believe her,' he said. 'All she *said* – but she has a secret, Jerry – she has a secret – everyone seems to have a secret. The murdered man must have been a most extraordinary customer. I wonder – '

His remark was cut short by a sudden nervous rap on the door, which burst open the next instant as a man in an invalid chair shot into the room.

He darted forward right up to the table at which the detective sat, and put out his hand and grasped the ledge to steady himself. As he did so he showed only head and shoulders high above the board. And as they sat looking at him the same thought flashed simultaneously into the minds of both father and son ... the gun on the table, the scorched tablecloth ...

The shot that killed Eric Crowther could only have been fired by a man or woman kneeling ... or sitting ...

4 The Invalid Chair

'You sent for me?'

W.T. looked at the man steadily, and his eyes seemed to become brighter and very piercing.

'You are Roger William Christensen,' he began, 'the owner of the house?'

'Yes.' The monosyllable was quietly spoken.

'Where were you at the time of the murder?' The cripple's grave face was unmoved by any tremor of emotion.

'I was in the drawing-room,' he said – 'the room next to this one, that is, in between this and the dining-room.'

'You can prove that, of course?' W.T.'s tone was dry and matter of fact. The man looked faintly surprised.

'Why, no,' he said, laughing deprecatingly. 'I don't suppose I can. I was quite alone, looking through my books in there, waiting for my wife to come in to tea. The books are as I left them when I heard the shots. I don't know if that would be any sort of proof.'

W.T. ignored the last remark. He was busy jotting down notes in the unofficial-looking memo book he always carried.

'When you heard the shot,' he went on at last, 'what did you do?'

'I hurried out into the hall – naturally – the report was terrific.'

'Quite,' said the detective, without looking up. 'You must have been the nearest to the scene. Were you the first to make the discovery?'

'No, as it happens I was not.' The man spoke easily, in a quiet conversational tone, his drawn face the only indication of any strain he may have felt. 'I always have some difficulty in negotiating a door that opens inwards – that is to say towards me. As you see, I am pretty helpless in this chair' – he laughed a little awkwardly. 'I believe I was some seconds longer than usual in getting the drawing-room door open on this occasion,' he went on. 'The explosion had made me nervy, I suppose. When I did get into the hall I found Kathreen there, and the next instant my wife dashed out of the dining-room doorway screaming and crying that Crowther was murdered.'

He paused, and W.T. frowned.

'If you don't mind, Mr Christensen,' he said, 'I'll have the girl Kathreen in to verify that now.'

The cripple bowed.

'Anything you wish,' he said.

The old detective looked at his downcast eyes and resigned expression with the eye of an expert. For a moment he was silent, then he turned to the red-headed policeman.

'Send Kathreen Goody in, constable,' he said, and waited in silence until the man returned with the plump, round-faced girl that he and Jerry had carried in from the road.

She was still terrified, and her brown eyes were almost circular.

All W.T.'s benign, avuncular manner returned at the sight of her distress, and he beamed upon her.

'Now, Kathreen,' he said, 'I want you to try hard to remember what happened this afternoon. You spent most of the time up in the spare room with Miss Phillips sorting linen – did you?'

'Ye-e-s,' said Kathreen, with a great effort.

'Good,' said W.T., smiling. 'And what did you do next?'

'I – I come downstairs to get tea,' said Kathreen, 'and I went into the pantry to get the butter and – ' She broke off huskily and began to shake.

'And I heard the bang, sir.'

'Yes?' said the detective, with that patience for which he was noted.

'Yes – and what did you do then?'

Kathreen pulled herself together.

'I – I said "Oh!" sir, and dropped the butter,' she said huskily.

The old detective's expression did not change.

'Very naturally,' he said pleasantly. 'And did you go straight into the hall after that?'

'No, sir,' said Kathreen. 'Cook made me pick up the butter first.'

'Oh, Cook was there too, was she?'

'Yes, sir.'

'When you heard the shot?'

'Yes, sir.'

'About how long was it after you heard the shot that you went into the hall – three minutes?'

Kathreen hesitated.

'I dropped the butter first, sir – then I ran to the pantry door. Then Cook sent me back to pick up the butter. I did pick it up, and put it on to a clean plate; then I ran through the kitchen into the hall. It must have been about three minutes, sir.'

'Good girl,' said the detective. 'And when you reached the hall what did you see?'

'I saw the master edging his chair out of the drawing-room door, sir,' said the girl. 'Then the dining-room door burst open and Mrs Christensen came out screaming. I went into the dining-room, sir, and – ' Her brown eyes dilated with horror, and she grew inarticulate.

'That's all right, that's all right, Kathreen,' said the detective hastily, 'that's all I wanted to know. You can go now. Jerry, open the door for Miss Goody. That's all right, my girl – don't worry. Don't think of what you saw. It's all over now.'

If ever Jerry bundled a woman out of a room he considered he did it then. He was afraid that she was going to faint again, and he saw her safely seated in the drawing-room with relief.

Norah was in there too, seated near the fireplace. She smiled at him a little wanly as he came in, and he was just about to cross the room to speak to her when his eyes fell on a door in the wall that separated the drawing-room from the dining-room. He had not noticed it from the other side. It must open into the dark corner behind the heavy window-curtains, he reflected.

The man in the invalid chair had been in the drawing-room

at the time of the murder. On his own admission it was three minutes after the shot before he came out into the hall. Might he not have spent that three minutes in darting back through this second doorway and getting himself across the room to the other into the hall? In the face of Estah's story – in the face of the scorched tablecloth – in the face of Mrs Christensen's admission of her husband's jealousy – there seemed at that moment no other explanation of the mystery.

Jerry pointed to the door and strove to speak naturally.

'I say,' he said, 'does that door open?'

Norah looked up at him with surprise.

'Of course it does,' she said. 'Why?'

'It's – it's not kept locked?' persisted Jerry.

The girl leant across from her seat, and, turning the handle, pulled the door open.

'See?' she said. 'It's always left like that. We use it often.'

Jerry did not answer her. He was so overcome by his discovery that he turned on his heel abruptly and hurried back to the morning-room, leaving her staring after him.

'Of course,' W.T. was saying, as Jerry re-entered the room and silently took up his old position behind the older man's chair, 'of course, Mr Christensen, the girl's story bears out yours very well, but there is a matter concerning your wife that I am afraid I must ask you to discuss with me, because up to now the evidence upon it has been greatly at variance – '

The cripple looked at him steadily.

'Don't hesitate to ask me anything,' he said.

'Had you ever any cause to think that your wife was receiving attentions from Eric Crowther?'

The cripple raised his eyes slowly and looked the detective full in the face.

'No,' he said at last.

W.T. hesitated a moment, and Jerry's mind went back to Estah Phillips' vivid story of the conversation she had overheard from the balcony. W.T. must have been thinking of it also, for he said:

'I'm sorry to have to talk like this, Mr Christensen, but did nothing the dead man ever said to you suggest that there was some sort of – well – intrigue going on?'

The man in the invalid chair paused for a moment before replying, and an expression of loathing and contempt passed over his face.

'The dead man was the most despicable wretch on the face of this earth!' he said. 'Sometimes I thought he must be mad – then I forgave him a little.'

There was silence in the room after he had spoken, and the echo of his words seemed to cling and hang about the atmosphere, although they had not been spoken in anything approaching a loud voice.

W.T. was the first to speak after this announcement.

'I'm afraid you will have to explain, Mr Christensen,' he said slowly.

The cripple nodded, and his long thin fingers twisted and untwisted themselves with nervous haste.

'Eric Crowther was a coward and a bully,' he said. 'From the day I returned from France crippled as you see me now, he has come striding into my house as if he had a right here – insinuating her infidelity – gently at first – almost imperceptibly, then openly – bragging, gesticulating, *lying.*'

His voice died away to a whisper, and the old detective stared at him with surprise.

'Lying?' he murmured.

'Of course!' The cripple's tone was contemptuous.

The detective spoke again.

'If you knew he was lying I don't quite see why you put up with him,' he said, 'especially as you seem to have resented his intrusion.'

'I had to put up with him.' Roger Christensen's tone was still quiet, but the passion of resentment showed beneath the forced calm. 'What else could I do?' he went on. 'He was not a man upon whom words had the least effect. He was without decency – without pride. My natural protection was the police, I suppose – I might have prosecuted him for trespass or annoyance, but I shrank from that – my wife dreaded the publicity – she hated

Crowther as much as I did, but she would never discuss him, and I never pressed her.' He paused, and a bitter smile twisted his wide, sensitive mouth. 'The only right way to deal with a man like that was to whip him,' he said, 'and you see I was incapacitated from taking that way . . . God! What I would have given for my old strength just for an hour!' The last sentence burst from his lips involuntarily.

The detective frowned.

'I must warn you you're making some very dangerous statements, Mr Christensen,' he said gently. 'Do you quite realize the importance of them?'

The man nodded.

'I said I should tell you all I knew,' he said slowly. 'I did not kill Crowther, but if I had I should only feel ashamed that I could not have thrashed him first. I was in the drawing-room until the shot was fired; then I behaved exactly as I have told you.'

The detective sighed.

'Well, Mr Christensen,' he said, 'that will do for the moment, but I must ask you not to leave the house.'

The cripple nodded.

'I quite understand,' he said, and wheeling round in his chair, he passed out through the door that Jerry held open for him, into the hall beyond.

'Now,' said W.T. as the door closed. 'I think we'll adjourn for the night.'

As might be imagined, the inspector and the red-headed policeman raised no objections and within ten minutes Jerry and his father were alone.

5   The Only Alternative

'Well,' said the old man, looking across at his son, 'found the murderer, Jerry?'

The boy grimaced. 'It's pretty obvious, isn't it?'

W.T. raised his eyebrows. 'That poor devil in the chair is responsible,' said Jerry. 'Look here, Dad, this is how it happened ...'

Hastily he gave a short outline of the theory he had formed in his brief sojourn in the drawing-room. 'Did you notice that door?' he finished eagerly. 'It's always kept unlocked; the whole household use it. What could have been simpler than for the chap to nip in there, whip up the gun from the corner, fire from the table, and then bolt back again into the drawing-room and get out through the main door into the hall? It's as plain as print – he's given himself away.'

W.T. sighed.

'Jerry,' he said, 'you have a quick eye, a fertile imagination, and the gift of application, but you'll never make a detective – you've no ground-work. Did you notice anything about that door besides the fact that it wasn't locked?'

'No,' admitted Jerry, 'nothing particular – why?'

The old detective produced his memo book and turned over the pages.

'Here,' he said at last – 'here it is. That door, Jerry, is barely twenty-six inches across – and our friend Mr Christensen's chair is an exceptionally wide one. See his wheel-tracks on that sheet of newspaper on the floor down there – measure them for me.'

Jerry took the tape he proffered and went down on his hands and knees to obey him.

'Twenty-seven and a half inches,' he said at last.

W.T. nodded. 'And that's without the wheel-hubs,' he said. 'He couldn't have got through your door, Jerry – so bang goes that little theory, my boy. No, Roger Christensen's only way of committing that murder was to hurry out of the drawing-room as soon as he heard Crowther enter the hall, get past the man on the other side of the table, take the gun from the corner, kill him, and then double back out of the dining-room, taking care to avoid the body, which lay right across the inside of it – a very ticklish piece of work – and then hurry through the hall and back into the drawing-room, all before Kathreen arrived on the scene – she saw him coming out of the room, not going *into* it, remember. Pretty sharp work for a man hampered with a chair in three minutes, eh? The girl told us he had to "edge" his way through the drawing-room door as it was. By the way, you'll notice if you look that all the door-frames in the house are scratched where he passes in and out of them. No, Jerry, my boy, I don't think that's our man.'

Jerry sat back on his heels and looked at his father – his natural expression of faint bewilderment intensified.

'Then who – who ... ?' he began.

W.T. nodded and passed his hands over his shaggy white head. 'That's just the point. They all behave as if they were innocent, and yet each one is hiding something. Each has a motive for killing Crowther, and admits it freely. No sane person would dare to do that unless they felt safe. Let's take them one at a time. There's Mrs Christensen. She found the body – that is to say she was the first person seen coming from the room where the body lay. She admits freely – that's the devil of it – that she hated Crowther and her life was made unbearable by him. He came over here today to see her – we know that ... Then she says that her husband was jealous of the man – and we afterwards find that to be untrue. She was hiding something – some secret that she shared with Crowther, the nature of which we do not yet know.'

The detective paused and eyed his son. 'So far things look very black against her,' he went on, 'but I swear that her cry when she realized the inference I was drawing from her words was one of *surprise* as much as of horror; and then again she sent for the child – *she* sent for it, mark you, not I – and it destroyed her only alibi.

'Then there is her husband.' W.T. frowned as he spoke. 'On the face of the facts – the gun being where it was and this admitted hatred – he might quite as easily have done it as his wife. Yet apart from the difficulties of time and movement I am inclined to believe his story on its own account – it sounded true.'

Jerry nodded. 'It did,' he agreed. 'He really seemed to be trying to help.'

W.T. smiled wryly.

'That's often a sign of guilt,' he said. 'When a man says he is anxious to help and tells us long yarns about other people, he's usually hiding something. This fellow talked all about himself, though, which was odd if he was guilty.'

'Then there's Estah,' said Jerry.

'I know,' said the detective. 'There's another problem. Estah might have killed Crowther – nothing is more likely. She hated him – she tells us he ought to be dead – she even goes so far as to say that she prayed that he might die – there is no one to prove what she was doing at the time of the murder. She even had just time after Kathreen left her to cross the upper hall to the nursery, come down the garden steps, enter the french windows and fire at the incoming Crowther, returning the way she came before Mrs Christensen hurried round the side of the house. All that is possible, I say, but on the other hand, is it probable? Why should she know the exact moment when Crowther entered the house? Her window overlooked the garden. Why should she fire the gun from the table? Whoever committed that murder must have done it on the spur of the moment; there was no time for a quarrel before the shot. On his own servant's evidence Crowther left his house at fifteen minutes past four; five minutes later he was dead. They all know something about it, Jerry, but we've no more proof of the actual murder against them than we have against Kathreen or that sister of Mrs Christensen's I spoke to, or that old rascal Clarry Gale, whose very presence is a mystery . . .'

Jerry sat silent for a moment or so, then he looked up gravely.

'And the only other alternative . . .' he began.

'Is Cellini,' finished W.T. 'We shall hear news of him soon – he's the most likely person now; and yet,' he added with a sudden explosive laugh – 'and yet if he hadn't bolted we shouldn't have any more evidence against him than we have against any of the others.'

Hardly had the words left his lips than the door opened to admit a man whose eyes peered at the world suspiciously from beneath bushy eyebrows. This was Evelyn Cave – one of the most useful medical men Scotland Yard possessed.

The detective rose to meet him. The two were good friends and had been on many cases together in their time.

'Nothing new, I suppose?' There was something approaching wistfulness in the detective's tone.

The doctor hesitated.

'Well,' he said. 'I don't know . . . The body did not fall as it was found. I suspected that at first, although it seemed natural enough that the fellow should fall flat on his back away from an explosion like that – but from various little evidences which I have since discovered I have now confirmed my first suspicion.'

W.T. stared at him.

'What do you mean?' he said sharply. 'The man rolled over after he touched the ground, or – someone moved him after he was dead?'

Doctor Cave thrust his hands deep in his pockets and raised himself on his toes, his head jerked back a little to survey his colleague's face.

'Someone moved him,' he said. 'Someone rolled him right over on his back. Come and have a look.'

Jerry followed his father and the doctor into the room where the blood-covered corpse still lay.

The sight of it turned the boy sick again, as it had done before, but the doctor and old W.T. bent over it curiously.

'You see,' Cave was saying, his calm ruffled a little in his enthusiasm – 'you see, Will, when he fell his right shoulder struck this dresser-leg, and that pitched him forward on to his face, which accounts for this great pool of blood here – he must have remained like that for several seconds bleeding like a pig the whole time. See, the stain spreads all round him – had he fallen on his back the blood must have remained for the most part in the body.'

Jerry turned away, his gorge rising, but the detective leant forward, his eyes narrowing and the lines on his broad forehead deepening.

'I see,' he said slowly. 'Then you think someone turned him over after he fell – someone who – who wanted to see his face, for instance? . . .'

'Yes,' said Cave simply, 'or someone who wanted to get at his breast pocket.'

For a moment there was silence after the doctor had spoken. At last the detective straightened himself and paced slowly down the room.

'Nothing was missing though,' he said. 'The notecase was found intact save for the shot-holes – the body was not robbed of money . . .'

'Yet I believe it was robbed,' the doctor persisted. 'Look at the way this shirt is torn – it is so saturated with blood that I didn't notice it at first – but no shot-gun made a rip like that – that was *torn* open.'

W.T. nodded. 'You're right, Cave,' he said quietly. 'This makes all the difference . . . It was no ordinary robbery. The murderer wanted something Crowther kept very carefully – something that he was so afraid of losing that he kept it buttoned under his shirt – now at last I think we're coming to something, thank God.'

Once again he relapsed into silence.

'Of course,' he said. 'Of course – naturally.'

'What?' said Jerry, who was bewildered by this new development and the possibilities it suggested.

'Why,' said W.T., 'whoever moved that body after the shot was fired must have had his – or her – hands covered with blood. There is no other alternative – the cleverest creature alive could not have wrenched open that shirt and extracted a package from the man's breast without being contaminated – you can see for yourself it's impossible. That brings us nearer to facts at once. Within three minutes of the shot the entire crowd of suspects were gathered together in the hall. Bloodstains are not easy to hide, and the chances are a hundred to one against anyone getting away with them unnoticed at a time when everyone is instinctively looking at his neighbour and asking, "Is it you?"'

'Not everyone,' said Jerry suddenly. 'Not everyone was in the hall, Dad.'

W.T. nodded.

'That's it,' he said. 'Cellini ... No one saw him in the house, though, mind you. You fancied he turned in at the gate after he passed you but you didn't see him – you can't prove it. The cook at the "Dene" says he came into the house and went off again in the car after Clarry Gale had come over here – that was after the inspector arrived – quite fifteen minutes after the crime ... If he came here, as you fancied, where was he during that fifteen minutes between the shot and the moment when he returned to the "Dene" and was seen by the cook?' He was silent for a moment, and then went on again, speaking in a slow, meticulous way as if he were thinking each word out for himself for the first time.

'He was not in here,' he said. 'There is nowhere here for him to hide, and Mrs Christensen entered the room from the french windows almost immediately after she heard the shot. No, he must have gone out of the door – not having time to wipe his hands or to examine the package, or whatever it was that he had taken from the body. Kathreen did not see him as she came from the kitchen. Did he go out of the open front door, then, on to the veranda – or ... ?' He paused and looked at Jerry and the doctor.

'I think,' he said suddenly, 'that I shall make a detailed examination of the hall. I've been round this room and there's no sign of anything unusual, but the hall I have not yet had the opportunity to examine thoroughly. I had it photographed, but that was all. I thought it was going to prove such an ordinary case.' He sighed on the last word, and Cave smiled.

'Losing your dash, Will?' he said slyly.

The old detective grimaced at him.

'None of us gets younger,' he grumbled, 'and I never did like my job – spending one's life prying into other people's affairs – faugh!'

The doctor laughed – to Jerry's somewhat nerve-stricken imagination he looked like some odd ghoul in the yellow light.

'Oh, I enjoy my work,' he said, speaking the verb as if he meant it. 'They'll have to carry me to cases in a bath-chair when I'm too old to walk to them – I shall never give up.'

W.T. sighed.

'Every man to his taste,' he said. 'Jerry, my boy, in my coat in the next room you'll find my torch – bring it to me, will you?'

When Jerry returned with the torch, W.T. was standing before the miscellaneous collection of coats and mackintoshes that every English family seems to accumulate somewhere near its front door. The stand was set across the corner of the room between the dining-room door and the veranda. It was heavy with a mirror at the top and umbrellas at the bottom.

W.T. pulled aside the bundle of coats that draped the near side of the mirror.

'Look,' he said.

The stand, which by the overflowing burden of garments looked to be set close up against the wall, was, in fact, some eight inches away from it.

'A man could slip behind there easily,' said W.T. quietly, 'and out the other side again when the time came . . . Besides, see this?'

As he spoke he switched his torch on to the sleeve of the outermost coat, which until now had been hidden against the wall. Jerry caught his breath. There was a stain upon it – brown and sinister and unmistakable.

'It is new, too,' said W.T. 'And here also, see?'

Once again the torch's bright blade of light cut through the darkness of the corner and fell this time upon a spot on the wall about two and a half feet from the ground. There again was the same brown stain only more distinct this time – two oval smears of it side by side – one a little higher than the other. Fingermarks of a hand pressed lightly against the wall to preserve a man's balance as he flattened himself there.

Jerry looked at his father.

'Cellini!' he said faintly. 'He was there the whole time – waiting.'

W.T. nodded.

'As he came out of the dining-room he must have heard Kathreen coming, and so took shelter in this corner until he had an opportunity to escape. He must have been there until the inspector arrived and herded everyone into the drawing-room. Then he saw his chance and slipped out.'

Morning brought no news from the ports, and the detective was clearly disappointed. The inquest had been fixed for the following afternoon, and since they would both have to attend it, Jerry and his father spent the day in the village making what inquiries they could about the dead man.

The curious atmosphere of secrecy in the Christensen household also was too strong to be ignored. W.T. was puzzled.

'Cellini may have done the murder,' he said, 'but I can't help feeling that some interesting facts about all sorts of people will come to light before he is sentenced.'

Jerry sighed.

'I hope not,' he said involuntarily.

The older man smiled wryly.

'I know,' he said. 'That is often the real tragedy of a case like this. The whole of our civilization is one network of little intrigues, some harmless, others serious, all going on in the dark just under the surface. A crime calls the attention of the community to one point, and the searchlight of public interest is switched on to this particular section of the network. The trouble is that the light does not fall upon one spot alone, but shows up all the surrounding knots and tangles, making them out of all proportion by their proximity to the murder.'

'Foul!' said Jerry, whose thoughts were dwelling almost entirely upon Norah this morning, and they walked on in silence.

Inquiries in the village were not altogether helpful. The detec-

tive discovered little that he did not know already. The dead man
had not been liked by the countryfolk because, as they said,
'he kept himself to himself'. Of Cellini no one knew anything
save that he seemed to have followed his employer like a shadow,
the one hardly ever being seen abroad without the other.

The day passed without any discovery of any importance, and
W.T. began to get restless. He and Jerry were seated in the private
room in the 'Blue Boar', having their evening meal, when a
phone call disturbed them. W.T. left the table eagerly and returned five minutes later, a more satisfied expression on his face
than it had worn all day.

'At last,' he said, reseating himself, 'they've found the car.
Cellini left it in a Folkestone garage just before six o'clock last
night. A boat for Boulogne left the harbour at six-fifteen, and
Inspector Deadwood is of the opinion that he probably caught
it and got across before the general call was put out to the
ports.'

Jerry looked up.

'That's pretty serious, isn't it? I mean, there's not much
chance of getting him now, is there?'

'Oh dear me, yes!' W.T. was brightening up visibly, and the
gloom which had enveloped him all day now began to disperse
like fog before the sun. 'You can chase a man in one country as
well as another,' he said. 'The French police have been informed
of course, and will doubtless render us every assistance in their
power ... Feel like a trip to the Continent, Jerry?'

'Why, is it likely?'

'Very,' said the old man. 'I must get an extradition order.'

Late the following afternoon, as father and son walked back to
the 'Blue Boar' from the inquest they were met with a message.

Cellini located in Paris. French police report arrest impossible at the
moment. M. le Gris of the Intelligence Department will explain by
word of mouth alone. – Deadwood.

W.T. and Jerry exchanged glances.

'What does it mean?' the boy demanded, his forehead pucker-
ing.

W.T. thrust his fingers through his white hair till it stood up on his head like a cockatoo's crest.

'Goodness only knows,' he said. 'There's something very odd about this case, Jerry.'

6 The Explanation of M. le Gris

'If messieurs would permit ...' The tall fair-haired young Frenchman with the irreproachable English accent bowed deferentially as he spoke, and wafted rather than led the detective and his son into the sleek black car drawn up against the kerb outside the Gare du Nord.

He had met their train, and singling them out immediately from the other passengers, presented his card – M. Maurice Barthés, 18 rue des Soldats.

'I am Monsieur le Gris' private secretary,' he explained. 'He sends you this letter and begs that you will excuse him that he does not meet you himself.'

Old W.T. took the note and opened it, passing it immediately afterwards to Jerry.

My dear Mr Challoner, Would you be so good as to accompany my secretary to my house, where I shall await you? Please excuse this informality, but there are circumstances in the business on which you are come which make an unofficial meeting between us imperative.
René le Gris.

During the drive, which carried them through the heart of the city to the quiet squares on the other side of the river, M. Barthés talked continually upon trivial subjects. From his behaviour he might quite easily have been escorting two English business men to a house-party at the home of a member of an allied firm.

W.T. was not surprised. The boy was afraid of questions, he realized; he had been warned to say nothing, no doubt. This was understandable, but yet mystifying; and the old man sat silent, his hands folded.

Jerry therefore was left to bear the brunt of M. Barthés' small-talk, and the two young men chatted dutifully together for some fifteen minutes, until the car turned suddenly out of a noisy thoroughfare into a quiet old-fashioned avenue where the trees, green and dusty in the heat, nodded together before tall brown houses.

They came to a standstill before a house whose windows were hung with old-fashioned looped plush curtains and showed the gleam of polished mahogany in their shadowed depths.

A sedate manservant admitted them, leading them upstairs to a room on the first floor. Here M. Barthés paused and bowed.

'Monsieur le Gris awaits you, messieurs,' he said, and turning, left them on the threshold.

Jerry followed his father into a cool dim room whose atmosphere was redolent of leather and the faint dusty smell of books.

A slight figure rose from the shadows behind a desk as they came in, and moved towards them with outstretched hand.

M. René le Gris was a Frenchman of the dapper type. He was scarcely five feet six in height, with a grey vandyke beard, iron-grey hair, and black-brown eyes.

He smiled affably as he greeted the two, showing his perfect teeth, and reseated himself as soon as they sat down, drawing his chair nearer to theirs.

There was something about him, however, which made Jerry vaguely uncomfortable. There was a hint of restraint in his manner in spite of all his apparent friendliness.

W.T. noticed it also, and the faintly puzzled expression that had been lurking at the back of his eyes ever since he first set foot in Paris grew momentarily more intense.

The Frenchman was the first to touch on the business in hand.

'Monsieur,' he said, in his quiet, well-modulated voice, 'I understand from a letter I have received from London that you have come to France to find an Italian called Latte Cellini.'

W.T. nodded.

'I have come to arrest him, monsieur,' he said simply. 'We want him in England on a charge of murder.'

'So I understand,' said le Gris, and was silent for a moment or so, evidently deliberating his next remark.

'This is a very difficult matter,' he said at last. 'Monsieur knows, of course, that the French police are always most anxious to assist their colleagues over the Channel – '

W.T. bowed and was silent. This was all very well, but it was not to the point.

The little Frenchman folded his hands and smiled.

'This must all seem very extraordinary to you,' he said suddenly – 'asking you to come here unofficially like this.'

The old detective looked at him squarely.

'To be truthful, it does,' he said. 'I don't understand it at all. We hear from you that a man wanted on a charge of murder has been located in your city. Why can't we proceed in the ordinary way – as in the case of Chalmers – Ruth Buller – Dorrington, and many others?'

The Frenchman paused, and when at last he spoke there was an air of hesitancy in his manner, as if he were feeling his way very cautiously.

'Chalmers was a man in an ordinary position,' he said at last. 'So was the woman Ruth Buller – so was Dorrington. But Latte Cellini is not so ordinary. That is – I mean, monsieur, there are *circumstances* ...' And again he paused and looked at the Englishman questioningly.

W.T. remained stolid, however, his eyes fixed on the Frenchman's face. After a while the man continued.

'Monsieur,' he said, 'Latte Cellini is not unknown to us. He left France seven years ago, and since then all trace of him has been lost. Before that time, however, he was a subject of great interest to us. As soon as he entered France two days ago he was recognized by our men and a note made of his return. That is why we were able to reply to your inquiries about him so soon.'

W.T. nodded. 'I understand,' he said. 'But really, monsieur, I fail to see why the fact that seven years ago he was known to your police should prevent me from arresting him now.'

'Oh, my dear Monsieur Challoner, you misunderstand me.' M. le Gris was loud in his protest. 'We do not object at all to your arresting Cellini – even hanging him if you see fit; on the contrary, if you have sufficient evidence to bring him to justice there is nothing that would suit us more admirably. That is why – to be frank – we replied so promptly to your inquiries.'

W.T. stirred uneasily in his chair.

'Monsieur le Gris,' he said simply, 'I am an Englishman, and we like our facts like our food – without subtlety. If you will honour me with your trust you will find that I shall respect your confidence.'

The Frenchman coloured faintly.

'The affair is not easy,' he murmured. 'The facts, monsieur, are these – we know where Cellini is at the moment, but he is in a place where you cannot be permitted to arrest him. I can only suggest that you remain in Paris until we are able to give you more satisfactory information.'

W.T.'s eyes narrowed for an instant, but the next moment he was smiling, benign as ever.

'Monsieur,' he said gently, 'we are both servants of the established order. Let us work together. It seems to me that here is a man an offender against the public. If by cooperation we can bring him to justice, surely we ought to do so. In plain words, monsieur, let us each tell all we know.'

René le Gris frowned.

'Monsieur will understand the extremely confidential nature of the information for which he asks?' he said at last.

'My dear sir' – W.T.'s tone was eloquent – 'every police force in the world has its secrets. There are times when a strict adherence to the letter of the law is not advisable in the law's own interests.'

A faint smile spread over the little Frenchman's face. 'Monsieur comprehends,' he said, and then, turning, looked pointedly at Jerry.

'My son is my most valued assistant,' said old W.T. quickly. 'Please regard him as trustworthy as myself – I will answer for him.'

Le Gris shrugged his shoulders.

'As monsieur wishes,' he said, and leaning forward he began to speak, his elbows resting on his chair-arms, his white fingers meeting across his breast.

'As monsieur has said,' he began, 'every police force in the world has its secrets – information which it is not politic to use.' His bright eyes rested upon W.T.'s stolid face questioningly.

The old detective nodded emphatically and the Frenchman continued. 'We are not exceptions to the general rule. There has been for many years in this city the headquarters of a society of thieves. The police know of it, naturally, but always their hands have been tied.' Again he paused and looked at the Englishman shrewdly, and again the older man nodded gravely.

'The difficulty is a peculiar one,' le Gris went on. 'This "society" is composed of several American millionaires, one English nobleman, an Austrian whose name is famous all over the world, three Frenchmen, and one woman, whose names are so illustrious that even among friends it would be unwise to mention them. Besides – even we do not know the entire member roll.'

W.T. nodded imperturbably. 'I understand perfectly, monsieur,' he said. 'Please go on.'

'This society has one great peculiarity,' le Gris continued slowly. 'It never steals anything that can be bought.'

Jerry looked up in surprise, not grasping his meaning at first.

'Nothing that money will buy,' the Frenchman repeated. 'The members are all collectors of rare jewellery and pictures. If the object desired by any one of them is on the market, then he is bound to buy it, paying whatever may be asked for it without question; but if, on the other hand, the treasure is not to be got by just means and he is still anxious to get it, he calls in the help of this society and it is obtained for him.'

'Stolen?'

Le Gris shrugged his shoulders.

'Acquired,' he murmured gently. 'Wherever it is – the Imperial Palace of China or a back attic in your Mile End Road – it is found and removed. Nothing can save it.'

'The society has good servants,' remarked W.T.

The Frenchman nodded.

'All the experts of the world,' he said with something akin to regret in his tone. 'Every criminal who is at the height of his or her particular line is sought out and employed by them. Cracksmen – confidence men – pickpockets – besides a small army of jewellers and picture experts.'

The English detective looked up.

'I begin to understand,' he said. 'Latte Cellini was at one time in the employ of this society?'

Le Gris bowed. 'Monsieur is right,' he said. 'Latte Cellini is a jeweller – probably the most expert setter of precious stones in the world. He has been of great use to the society in the past. . .' He paused and smiled faintly, as if he were remembering something. 'There is today,' he said at last, 'amongst the Crown Jewels of a great Royal House a single false stone. The original lies in the collection of a famous American beside its only peer – a stone of the same colour, quality and weight. No one in the Royal household dreams of the exchange, since no one but an expert with a glass could tell the difference between the false stone and the real one. But twelve years ago all the jewellery was cleaned, and one night an old jeweller from Prague sat up late at the work – or so it was thought. The following morning the change had been effected. That was the work of Latte Cellini. But we could never prove it against him.'

'A worthy successor of his great namesake,' remarked W.T., who seemed to have relished the story.

Jerry frowned. 'Did he impersonate the jeweller from Prague, then?' he said.

Le Gris nodded.

'Gustav Buder of Prague did not receive his summons from the Royal Treasury,' he said. 'To this day he does not know that it was despatched.'

There was silence for a moment or so after the Frenchman's voice had died away. Then W.T. spoke.

'I understand the powers of this society, monsieur,' he said, 'but surely even it cannot protect a man wanted for murder.'

'But no, certainly not, monsieur.' Le Gris spoke emphatically. 'Besides, the society does not defend its servants. That is part of the agreement under which they are employed. They are paid enormous salaries on the condition that they take the full responsibility of their own actions. Besides, the society has its own methods of dealing with unsatisfactory servants.'

W.T. looked up sharply, for the first time a flicker of surprise passing over his face.

'How do you mean?' he said.

Le Gris shrugged his shoulders eloquently. 'They disappear, monsieur,' he said simply. 'For seven years we thought that some such fate had overtaken Latte Cellini, but two days ago he reappeared in Paris with the English police on his heels. Can you offer us any explanation?'

'Very little,' W.T. admitted. 'All we know for certain about Cellini is that for the last seven years he has been living with an Englishman in a Kentish village in the capacity of private secretary or confidential servant.'

'Impossible!'

W.T. smiled dourly. 'It doesn't sound true, I admit,' he said, 'especially after your most valuable information concerning his past, but these, as far as we know them, are the facts. The Englishman – Crowther – was murdered two days ago, and the evidence, although not absolutely conclusive, points very strongly to the Italian. You know where he is?'

Le Gris nodded.

'Yes, monsieur, I do,' he said. 'That is the trouble of it. I know where he is, but I cannot take you to him.'

W.T. frowned. 'I am afraid I misunderstand you,' he said a little stiffly.

Le Gris leant back in his chair, and his pale finely chiselled face looked like an ivory carving in the dusk.

'When Cellini returned to France, monsieur, I feel sure that he had no idea that he would be followed,' he said slowly, 'for his first move was to go straight to the house of the head of the society – a man whose name I beg you will not ask me to divulge. But believe me, an arrest in that house is an impossibility. For political as well as social reasons, monsieur, it would be unwise in the extreme. We have made our plans. To disturb anything now would be to impede the course of justice in the future. As long as Cellini remains actually under the protection of this society – under its roof – we can do nothing.'

W.T. hesitated.

'But surely, monsieur, if I might venture to suggest it, a word to the – ah – distinguished member of the society would result in the expulsion of Cellini from the household, and we could then proceed in the ordinary way.'

Le Gris sighed.

'That could be done,' he said, 'but we prefer not. The police like to assume, even in private, a complete ignorance of the society. When a man is in this particular house of which I speak he is to all intents and purposes out of the world altogether; monsieur must understand the situation.'

'I do,' said the old man. 'I do indeed, and I thank you, Monsieur le Gris, for your very valuable assistance; but what am I to do?'

'I was coming to that, monsieur.' Le Gris sat forward in his chair. 'There is in the Rue d'Aramis a little jeweller's shop kept by an old relative of Cellini's. The man is sure to return there. We will have the place watched, and as soon as he enters the doorway you shall be informed.'

W.T. bowed, but his eyes had by no means a satisfied expression in their depths.

'Meanwhile, I wait in Paris,' he said at last.

Le Gris smiled.

'Yes, monsieur,' he said. 'That is all I can suggest. But you will not have long to wait,' he went on, 'and at the earliest opportunity you can rely on us to assist you to our utmost ability.'

The two men shook hands.

'Monsieur, I am so much in your debt already,' said W.T. gravely, 'that I cannot fully express my deep appreciation of your courtesy. You can rely upon our respect for your confidence.'

Le Gris bowed. 'As soon as the necessary information comes through, monsieur, you shall be informed,' he said.

'How extraordinary!' said W.T., as he and Jerry walked down the leafy avenue together.

'What?' said Jerry.

Old W.T. sighed.

'The society,' he said. 'It's known to every police force in Europe, of course, though professional etiquette forbids one to admit it. Nothing can be done to end it. The police of the world are powerless against it. We can only get proof against the servants of the society – not the members themselves. Even the French Intelligence Department can do nothing. We shall have to wait for our man, my boy.'

7 No. 28 Rue d'Aramis

After ten days in Paris Jerry had not forgotten Norah Bayliss. On the contrary, he thought about her more often every succeeding day that he was away from her – wondered what was happening to her, if she had stayed by her sister, if he would ever see her again.

He was absorbed with this last question when he turned into the foyer of the hotel and walked through into the lounge. W.T. was seated in the far corner of the room looking offensively English, with a litter of tea-things on the table before him.

He looked up as Jerry came in and began to grumble before the boy had reached his side.

'I thought you were never coming,' he said peevishly. 'Have a cigarette.'

Jerry took the rebuke and the peace-offering.

'Any luck?'

'At last. 'Pon my soul, Jerry, I was thinking of sending home for my winter vests and digging in here for the rest of the year. But young Barthés was down here half an hour ago – Cellini is abroad again and they expect him to sleep at the jeweller's in the Rue d'Aramis tonight. At ten o'clock, therefore, you, I, and an *agent de police* will go and get him. I thought I'd have you with us. Heaven knows, you're better with your fists than your head.'

Jerry grinned.

'Why,' he said, 'd'you expect a rough-house?'

W.T. shrugged his shoulders.

'Probably,' he said. 'No one likes being hanged, you know – most of 'em make a fight for it. Le Gris seems to expect trouble, anyway. It may be only his politeness, of course, but as far as I

can hear, half the police force is going to surround that shop tonight – gendarmes in every doorway – gendarmes on each
window-sill – gendarmes sticking out of every chimney-pot.'

Jerry laughed.

'Oh, well,' said the boy, 'it's a blessing we're getting a move on
at last. What I want to know is why Cellini killed Crowther in
Christensen's house?'

W.T. grunted.

'What I want to know is what Crowther had on him that
Cellini waited seven years to kill him for.'

At twenty minutes to ten the affable M. Barthés returned with
an *agent de police* called Marbeuf. Neither was in uniform, and
after some few moments of conversation the four climbed into
the car and the chauffeur drove off at speed. After one of the
most thrilling journeys Jerry had ever experienced, they arrived
at the corner of an ill-lit and by no means odourless street in one
of the poorer quarters of the town.

'I think, monsieur, it would be best to alight here,' said M.
Barthés in his quiet voice. 'The shop is some eight doors down
on the left-hand side – Number twenty-eight.'

'Very well,' said W.T., whose spirits had been steadily reviving
during the last fifteen minutes or so. 'Are you coming, Jerry?'

Together the father and son and the two Frenchmen walked
down the pavement to where a single rod of yellow light fell from
a chink in a wooden shutter outside a shop window.

'Here we are,' murmured M. Barthés. 'Our men are posted
on all sides. Monsieur has but to summon them.'

'Good,' said W.T. and, striding up to the door, knocked on it.

There was a moment of waiting, while Jerry felt himself
sympathizing with the man somewhere in the shop – caught like
a hare in a circle of dogs.

Then footsteps sounded inside the house and there was the
noise of a bolt being drawn back. The next moment the door
opened, cautiously, and a shaft of light shone out upon the four
men on the pavement. A woman stood on the threshold, tall and
sallow-skinned, with black, dull dry hair knotted loosely at her
neck. Her frock was long and made of some light cotton material

printed with a bright pattern. She looked at them doubtfully, and when she spoke her French had a southern accent.

W.T. took his hat off and bowed to her with as much ceremony as if she had been an old-time marquise and he an emissary from the English Court.

'Madame,' he began in his best French, which was as English as his clothes, 'we have called to see Signor Latte Cellini – '

The woman looked at him sharply, a sudden hint of fear appearing in her dark eyes.

'Ze Inglis?' she said. 'What name, monsieur?'

W.T. presented his card.

'Wait,' said the woman, and turning, left them standing in the doorway while she hurried out of the room into the back of the house.

The four men stepped into the shop, and Jerry looked round him curiously. It was a jeweller's, with a glass-case counter in which were displayed cheap rings and watches, together with a collection of initial brooches – silver-gilt monstrosities with girls' names emblazoned on the fronts. Nothing extraordinary here, thought Jerry.

His reflections were cut short by the reappearance of the woman. To his surprise, all trace of alarm had vanished entirely from her expressive face. She smiled at W.T. pleasantly.

'You go up?' she enquired in her imperfect English, which she seemed to consider at any rate was better than the old detective's French. ''E wait for you.'

The two Frenchmen exchanged glances, and Jerry saw W.T.'s hand slip round to his hip pocket.

W.T. spoke first.

'We will follow you, madame.'

'Ver' well.' The woman was still smiling, and turned at once into the passage leading out of the shop.

They followed her cautiously. The house was old and full of corners. W.T. had taken the lead as a right. Jerry followed him closely, the others pressing behind.

To their astonishment, and to Jerry's disgust, nothing untoward happened. The woman led them up a narrow staircase to a back bedroom which had been furnished as a sitting-room. It was depressingly lit and the furniture, although in good taste, was decidedly shabby.

Latte Cellini stood by the square table in the centre of the room looking at them with more curiosity than anything else.

Jerry recognized him at once. He was the man he had seen pass down the road on the day that he had stood by his car talking to the constable. There could be no mistaking the tall attenuated figure and the lank grey chin.

W.T. glanced behind him; the woman had gone out and the door was closed.

The detective came forward and cleared his throat:

'You are Latte Cellini?'

'Yes – that is my name.'

'On the fourteenth of this month you left the "Dene", Brandesdon, Kent, England, suddenly, and came to France?'

'Yes.' The Italian spoke easily, almost carelessly.

'If it is the car – I tink I can explain,' he said. 'I – '

W.T. stared at him.

'The car?' he ejaculated, 'it's much more serious than that – you're wanted on the charge of murdering Eric Crowther.'

'Murder? I?'

The effect upon the man was instantaneous. His calm vanished and he stared at the detective in surprise. 'I?' he repeated. 'I, monsieur? It is impossible! There is some mistake … some terrible mistake! Murder! My God! – let me explain, monsieur – for the love of heaven let me explain.'

The old detective was shaken by Cellini's surprise.

'Murder!' the Italian repeated, and added, a blaze lighting up his dull eyes: 'But no, monsieur. Had I been capable of murdering that man I should not have waited seven years to do it.'

This remark, coming as it did so naturally, swayed the old detective in spite of himself. He turned to M. Barthés.

'Monsieur,' he said in an undertone, 'the evidence against this man is very strong, but it is not yet absolutely conclusive.

Do you think we might diverge from the ordinary official course in this case? Entirely unofficial, of course: no notes will be taken.'

M. Barthés bowed his sleek yellow head.

'Whatever monsieur thinks advisable,' he murmured, and added softly, 'So that it may be entirely unofficial, Monsieur Marbeuf and I will await you in the shop downstairs – should you need us you have but to call.'

W.T. smiled.

'That's very good of you, sir,' he said. 'If you wouldn't mind, that's just what I should like.'

M. Barthés bowed, smiled faintly, and wafted himself and the sturdy and somewhat disappointed Marbeuf out of the room and down the stairs.

The Italian, who had not caught the drift of the conversation, looked after them wildly.

'Are they going?' he demanded hysterically. 'Going before they have heard me. Shall I be dragged off to prison without being heard? What is to become of me? Why am I not allowed to explain?' His voice rose almost to a scream on the last word, and Jerry noticed his long, tapering fingers as they clutched nervously at the tablecloth . . . delicate, sensitive fingers.

Old W.T. sat down. He was at his most fatherly, and his expression was innocent and benign.

'Now, calm yourself,' he said, and his voice was soothing. 'Those gentlemen are waiting for me downstairs. If you would care to reserve your story for the Court to hear, I am quite ready, but if you wish to tell me anything now – here I am.'

The terrified Italian became visibly calmer under the influence of the unemotional voice, and suddenly he dropped into a chair by the table. For some moments he sat silent, his long ivory white hands clasped in front of him and his eyes dull and impenetrable.

At last his lips moved.

'I kill him? *I?*' he murmured, and a thin trickle of laughter escaped him. 'For seven years – seven years I long to kill him. I think and plan and dream of killing him, but always I am afraid. He know that; that is why he not fear me.'

Jerry glanced at his father – his eyes wide with astonishment. The old man signalled him to be silent, and looked across at the Italian.

'Go on,' he said softly.

The man hesitated.

'I – I didn't kill him,' he burst out. 'Whoever it was it was not I – I would never dare. I lived with him for seven years as a prisoner.'

Old W.T. was frowning: the mystery was not becoming clearer. He leant across the table and regarded the Italian steadily.

'Cellini,' he said, 'why did you bolt like that – suddenly?'

The Italian looked at him blankly.

'Because he was dead,' he said. 'Because at last I was free.'

'How did you know Crowther was dead?'

Cellini's reply was disarming.

'Because I saw him,' he said simply. 'I followed him into the house of the Christensens, as he bade me – as I entered the front door I heard the report. I rushed into the room . . .' He paused and lowered his eyes.

'Yes?' said W.T.

'Then,' said Cellini, 'I saw he was dead, and I knew I was free. Something sang in my brain – my one desire was to get away. I hurried out of the room the way I had come. As I reached the hall I heard someone coming. I did not wish to be seen lest I should be delayed. There was not time to get out of the door, so I hid behind the coat-stand – I was there for some time while the police came. Then as soon as the hall was clear I ran out into the garden and returned to my room, where I packed a bag. Then I took the car and went.' He paused and returned the detective's stare.

W.T. hesitated, then he spoke.

'There was blood on the wall behind the coat-stand, Cellini,' he said slowly.

The man's face paled visibly until his round eyes seemed to glow against the livid flesh.

'What did you take from the dead man?' W.T. continued. 'What did you turn him over on his back and wrench his shirt open to find?'

'You know?' The words were uttered in a stifled scream, and the Italian started up from the table, his expression a masterpiece of fear and amazement.

W.T. nodded wearily.

'Of course I know,' he said. 'Sit down.'

Cellini obeyed him; he was trembling.

'What was it?'

The Italian folded his arms on the table and hid his face on them.

'I can't,' he said piteously. 'I can't ... I ... daren't.'

There was no question that his anguish was sincere. The man had literally gone to pieces before their eyes.

For a minute W.T. let him remain there quiet, his face hidden. Then he spoke deliberately.

'Cellini,' he said, 'have you ever heard of the *Society of the Undenied*?' He spoke very softly, but the effect upon the Italian was electrical. He sat up at the table, his long, thin body rigid, his nostrils dilated like those of a frightened animal.

'Who are you?' he demanded, and his voice was breathy and out of control.

W.T. smiled at him, his eyes narrow beneath his thick white brows.

'I don't think there's any need to go into that,' he said gently. 'Let it be enough that I know.'

There was silence for a moment in the room while the Italian still stared at the detective.

Finally W.T. leant back in his chair.

'Now that we understand each other, let us go into the matter afresh,' he said easily. 'You see, my only desire is to find the murderer of Eric Crowther. I have in my pocket a warrant for your arrest on that charge, but if you tell me the truth I will listen to it. I give you one word of advice ... If you are innocent, do not be afraid to tell the whole truth. I am not likely to bring any charges against you save this one that I have mentioned.'

The Italian raised his heavy eyes and spoke wearily.

'I will tell you,' he said.

8   The Torturer

Once having made up his mind to speak, the Italian's whole attitude changed as completely as it had done before. His weariness left him – he became voluble, excited. As he talked he gesticulated, his sensitive hands emphasizing his points – driving them home.

'Monsieur,' he said, 'seven years ago, in the service of the society by which I was employed, it became necessary for me to spend some months in a tenement building in the worst quarter of this city . . .' He paused and looked at the old detective keenly. 'I had to wipe out my own personality and become for a time a beggar in the streets of Paris – a real beggar. I lived on what I earned. I spoke to no one whom I knew in my own life – not even my wife . . . not even she would have recognized me.'

'Your wife? Is that the lady who showed us in?' Jerry spoke involuntarily.

The Italian nodded.

'Yesterday I saw her for the first time for seven years,' he said simply. 'But monsieur shall hear . . . However one can disguise the body and force the mind into a new shape and quality, one cannot control one's powers of resisting disease. The beggars of Paris live hard lives. From children they are inured to cold but I was not – I became ill.' He stopped for a moment and regarded W.T. solemnly.

The detective nodded comprehendingly, and the Italian went on. 'I caught some cold which laid me open to an attack of fever brought by another beggar from the East. It overcame me completely. I dare not return to my home, however, for I knew I was being watched, and bring suspicion upon the society I dare not . . . as you will understand, monsieur?'

'Yes,' said W.T., 'I understand.'

The Italian looked at him gratefully. 'So I crawled back to my tenement attic,' he continued, 'and lay upon my bed. Then began the tortures of long fits of delirium, from which I used to awake gasping with fear, icy cold and convinced in my mind that I was about to die. This misery continued for some time – how long I never knew – it may have been days or merely hours. But as I awakened from one of the worst fits of delirium, my mind frozen with the fear of death and the purgatory to come, I saw a man bending over me. A big man, wide-shouldered and heavy-faced, with small bright eyes round and cruel and a little mad ...'

He paused, and W.T. spoke. 'That was Eric Crowther?'

The Italian nodded, and there came into his face the same indescribable expression of mingled fear and loathing that Jerry had noticed on the faces of Christensen and Gale and old Estah when they had spoken of the dead man.

'It was he,' he said. 'The devil in man's guise. But I will tell you – you shall judge. When I saw him I cried out to him that I was dying, and he nodded. I was terrified – I am a member of the true Church, monsieur – a good Catholic, and in the hour of death I was afraid to die unabsolved. I begged him therefore to fetch a priest to me, and in my madness I said there was much I had to confess. I can see his face now as he looked at me. I was very ill, monsieur; mad with fever and the awful fear of dying with my sins unconfessed.'

The man was speaking passionately, his dull eyes glowing, and the two men who listened had a sudden insight into his superstitious soul. They saw a little of his belief – his faith that absolution would protect him from the fire and everlasting torment of the damned.

'He laughed at me,' the Italian continued, his voice sinking into a monotone. 'I saw him grinning down at me. "There is not time," he said. "You will die before he comes." This was the one thing needed to drive the last sane thought out of my mind. I became raving – hysterical – and he – as though to quiet me – suddenly offered to hear my confession. "I will be secret," he said, "and I will pray for you."' Cellini paused to draw breath for a moment, but went on again immediately, his words gathering speed. 'I was mad,' he said; 'the fever had heated my brain until I could think of nothing clearly; my whole being was frozen with the terror of death. I confessed,' he added slowly, while W.T. stared at him, a glimmer of understanding in his face. 'I confessed everything.'

W.T. stirred, and his voice sounded dry and quiet after the Italian's emotional outburst.

'About the society?'

Cellini bowed his head.

'I thought they were my last words on earth,' he said after a pause. 'I looked upon him as a confessor. I was too ill to ...'

W.T. nodded.

'And then?' he said.

'He took it down.' The Italian spoke so simply that for a moment Jerry did not grasp the full significance of the words.

'He took it down,' Cellini repeated, a gathering hatred in his tone. 'I spoke haltingly, naturally, for I was very weak – there was plenty of time for him to write, and when he had done he made me sign.'

W.T. stared at the man before him, his eyes narrowed with incredulous amazement.

'He made you sign?' he repeated.

The Italian nodded. 'I was ill,' he said gently. 'Dying – and I was afraid.'

The old detective leant back in his chair and folded his arms. He was beginning to see things more clearly.

'What exactly had you confessed?'

'Everything,' said the Italian.

W.T. frowned. 'Names?' he inquired.

'Everything,' repeated Cellini, and his tone told more than the most elaborate explanation could have done.

W.T. whistled softly.

'I see,' he said gravely. 'I see. And then – you didn't die.'

The Italian nodded.

'He saved my life,' he said. 'I never forgave him for that. He was a monster, monsieur – a fiend unleashed.'

W.T. rose to his feet, and crossing over to the hearth-rug stood there, his hands in his pockets.

'You must go on,' he said at last. 'All this you have told me only compromises you more.'

The Italian nodded eagerly. 'I know,' he said, 'I know. There is still more to explain. But yet – monsieur did not know the dead man – perhaps he could not understand.'

'Suppose you try to tell me,' said W.T. 'If it's true I shall understand.'

The Italian leant his elbows on the table and rested his chin on his hands. His unnatural pallor and dry, longish black hair gave him a weird, almost ghost-like appearance in the yellow light.

'Monsieur,' he began, 'Eric Crowther, though in all other respects an ordinary, self-centred, middle-aged man of rather fine intellect, was, on one point, mad – insane.' He looked across at the detective doubtfully, as if he feared he would not be believed, but W.T. regarded him solemnly, nothing but a deep interest betrayed in his expression. The Italian went on, still speaking more slowly than his wont, and with a meticulousness of diction that betrayed his anxiety to be understood.

'He had a mania,' he said, 'a passion for inflicting pain. Pain interested him. He loved to cause it, to watch his victim writhing, realizing and enjoying to the full with a sensuous pleasure each little twinge and stab.'

W.T. bowed his head.

'I am familiar with that type of obsession,' he said.

The Italian glanced at him sharply. 'You will understand, then,' he said, 'that was Crowther's madness, but he had it with a difference – the only pain that interested him was *mental* pain.'

Jerry caught his breath and leant forward.

'*Mental* pain,' the Italian repeated. 'He had studied medicine in Germany and was a great student of the brain – any kind of mental suffering thrilled him. At first it was just a secret trait in his character, I think, but it grew into a mania. At the time of which I speak his whole life was dominated by it as a man is dominated by a fiend.'

Both W.T. and Jerry were alert now, watching him eagerly. This revelation explained much that had been hitherto incomprehensible.

'It was difficult for him to gratify this mania,' the Italian continued. 'One must inspire love first before one can hurt with a word or a look; or else one must know something about someone – something they are anxious not to reveal to the world. Then one can play upon the feelings of the victim as a child plays upon a guitar . . .'

'My God – blackmail!' Jerry spoke without knowing it.

Cellini looked at him and nodded.

'That is the word,' he said. 'Blackmail – blackmail with the payments in pain.'

Jerry looked at his father questioningly. The old man was looking intently at the Italian, his forehead puckered and his face animated with new interest.

'Go on,' he said.

'Crowther used to find out about people,' Cellini continued, lowering his voice. 'He used to look for people who had secrets, get them into his power and then keep them under his eye, torturing them and holding over their heads continuously the threat of exposure.'

'What an unpleasant type!'

The Italian turned.

'You don't believe me!' he said quickly. 'But it's true – his household was composed of his victims – he used to go and live near people who were afraid of him.'

W.T. opened his mouth to ask a question, but thought better of it.

Cellini continued.

'He had a hold over me, anyway,' he said. 'Else why did I live with him all those years – a virtual slave – subjected to every indignity – forced to follow him about, to obey his every injunction unquestioningly? Monsieur, I dared not leave him – he had my signed confession – a paper which, if it had got into the hands of the society, would put me in danger of my life or worse.'

W.T. expelled a breath hissingly through his teeth.

'I see – I see,' he said. 'And he would threaten you with exposure from time to time?'

'Always. I was never for one moment at peace. I used to think of killing him – but I was afraid. I dared not.'

W.T. returned to his seat at the table.

'Look here, Cellini,' he said. 'I am indebted to you for this information about the dead man, but nothing you have said as yet has done anything to convince me that you did not kill him – in fact, all your story so far has simply added to my belief in your guilt ... If you turned and fled as soon as you saw that Crowther was lying dead on the ground, how did your hands come to have blood on them?'

'Ah, but, monsieur, don't you understand?' The Italian's tone was eager, and his brown eyes wide and pathetic. 'I turned him over – I took my confession.'

The old detective passed his hand through his white hair.

'You took your confession,' he repeated. 'Naturally, naturally.'

'But yes, monsieur.' Cellini's sincerity was unmistakable. 'When I heard the shot, and came rushing into the room to find him lying on his face dead, my first thought was of my confession – he always carried it about with him, I knew – I could not let it be found on him. I turned him over – psha! He was not good to look at – I had just time to wrench open his shirt, take out the leather case and fly. It was because of this that I was not quick enough to get out of the house before the maid came into the hall.'

W.T. bowed his head over his hands.

'My God!' he said. 'I almost believe you.'

Cellini sat up stiffly in his chair.

'I swear to you that I speak the truth,' he said slowly, and added, with a sudden burst of eagerness, 'Consider, monsieur – why should I kill him in another man's house, and with a gun – my natural weapon is the knife – I can throw a knife so as to hit a mark on the wall twenty feet away – I should have killed him like that had I dared. Besides – ask yourself – should I have waited seven years to do it?'

W.T. rose to his feet and walked slowly down the room, his hands clasped behind him, his head bowed.

'Cellini,' he said, turning suddenly, 'stay in Paris at this house. What you have said tonight has shaken my theory of your guilt but I am not yet satisfied.'

The Italian stood up.

'Monsieur, I assure you,' he said. 'I remain here. When you want me, this address will find me.'

'Splendid.' W.T. picked up his hat and turned towards the door. On the threshold he looked back.

'By the way, Cellini,' he said, 'you came into the room almost directly after the shot was fired, didn't you?'

'Within three seconds, monsieur.'

'Then did you – did you by any chance catch a glimpse of the firer of the shot – as he or she disappeared out of the french windows?'

Cellini hesitated.

'No, monsieur,' he said at last.

W.T. turned back into the room.

'What did you see?'

'I saw – nothing.'

W.T. shook his head.

'You make it very difficult for me,' he said. 'You see, it is my duty to find out all I can about this case – the sooner the guilty person is discovered the sooner will the innocent be out of danger of suspicion. What did you see?'

Again the Italian hesitated.

'I am not sure,' he said finally. 'It was not so much a glimpse as an impression – a thing that was gone so quickly that I could not swear that it had ever been.'

'I understand,' said the detective. 'What was your impression?'

The Italian raised his eyes and looked at the old man steadily.

'A flicker of white round the window-post,' he said slowly. 'A corner of white material.'

'Such as an apron edge?' suggested W.T. 'Or a woman's white petticoat?'

'Or a woman's white petticoat,' agreed the Italian. 'That was my impression, monsieur.'

As he closed the door of the room behind the two of them, Jerry murmured to his father:

'What are we going to say to Barthés and Marbeuf?'

9 Two Extravagant Ladies

At a little past eleven o'clock the following morning Jerry and his father walked down the sunlit Boulevard des Italiens discussing the affairs of the preceding night. When they had finally parted with the imperturbably polite M. Barthés and the covertly amused Marbeuf, W.T. had been in no mood for conversation. Now, however, he was more reconciled to the situation.

'I shall have Cellini watched, of course,' he was saying. 'Keep in touch with him – but somehow I'm inclined to believe in his story. That particular form of madness is not so rare and, besides, it is the only thing which explains to my mind the extraordinary case of Clarry Gale.'

'Clarry Gale – why shouldn't he have suddenly turned straight?'

W.T. shook his head. 'My boy,' he said solemnly, 'there are men who commit crime from weakness – from sudden temptation – from fear or from sheer necessity. All these may suddenly reform and go straight: but there is another type that is born with a twist – a criminal by nature – fundamentally crooked. Such a man is Clarry Gale. His record starts at the age of seven. He has spent twenty-five years of his sixty-three in prison. This ten years of blameless life doesn't seem natural somehow.'

Jerry nodded. 'He wouldn't talk, would he?' he said.

'No.' W.T. frowned. 'I had a long chat with him on the morning of the inquest, but he wouldn't say a word. He knew his alibi was all right, and traded on that. I couldn't get anything out of him.

'No, Clarry Gale was kept honest by a fear of his life. Crowther had some hold over him – that's why I'm inclined to believe

Cellini's story of the "mental torture and blackmail" business. It fits in so well.'

Jerry shrugged his shoulders expressively.

'*Not* good,' he said. 'I suppose our next move is to go back to ... Good lord!' Jerry stopped dead in his sentence and in his stride.

'What's the matter?'

'Norah!' said Jerry, and set off down the pavement at full speed.

W.T. looked after him; the next moment he too was staring down the road, genuine surprise in his face.

An open taxi-cab was drawn up outside a perfumer's some ten yards farther down the pavement. One woman was seated inside it, while another stood talking to Jerry.

They were Mrs Christensen and Norah.

The two young people were chatting together eagerly when W.T. came up, while Mrs Christensen was smiling on them happily.

To the old man's surprise, and somewhat to his embarrassment, she welcomed the two of them as old friends.

'We don't know a soul in this city – how jolly running into you! Are you doing anything at the moment? We're just going back to the hotel to eat. Won't you come with us?' Mrs Christensen spoke eagerly. She seemed really pleased to see them, and her smile was as ingenuous as her words.

W.T. looked at her, his face betraying no hint of the surprise he felt. She was a different woman from the haggard and terrified creature with the hunted look in her eyes that they had left in England only a few days before. She looked years younger, and there was colour in her cheeks and a new vivacity in her face. The detective's curiosity was aroused, and within minutes he had accepted her invitation and the four of them were rattling away down the rue de la Paix to the Place Vendôme.

Jerry and Norah were getting on well together, and W.T. turned his entire attention to Mrs Christensen. There was no need to question her, he found: she chattered on about herself without any encouragement.

'I felt I just must get away,' she said, 'if only for a week or so – so we're going down south to Mentone for a rest.'

'You – er – left your address, of course?' In spite of himself, the detective could not refrain from the question.

The woman stared at him as if she fancied he had taken leave of his senses.

'Of course I did,' she said. 'You see, my husband isn't with us.'

'No?'

'He was afraid of the journey,' she said. 'It was awkward for him, poor dear, in that chair.'

'Quite.' W.T. smiled at her. 'And so you came away without him?'

The woman nodded.

'I just packed Estah and the baby off to Bournemouth, sent Roger to his sister's house in Yorkshire, and Norah and I came over here. We only arrived yesterday. We shall spend the afternoon buying, and then tomorrow we start for Mentone.' She clapped her hands and laughed as she finished speaking, and W.T., looking at her, had the impression that she was set free – a linnet out of a cage. The whole affair puzzled him, though; he did not understand this new spirit, and there was the money too. The White Cottage was an unpretentious house – the Christensens were unpretentious people, living frugally on invested capital, no doubt. But Mrs Christensen now exuded an atmosphere of extravagance. Both she and Norah were very expensively dressed. W.T. had a pretty shrewd knowledge of the cost of clothes – it was part of his business – and he realized at once that the lady had been shopping already, and extravagantly at that.

The hotel, too, he found when they arrived, was one of the most exclusive and expensive in the city. The two sisters had a private suite and had brought their English maid with them, the bashful Kathreen, now considerably more perky and sure of herself.

Food was served in the suite, and the sisters chatted throughout the meal. It was their first visit to Paris, and they were full of their experiences. As far as W.T. could hear, they had made the best of their time. The general impression they gave him was one of feminine extravagance in its most reckless mood. The more he thought of it the more mystified he became.

He glanced at Jerry, but if he expected any confirmation of his impression from him he was disappointed. The boy was engrossed in conversation with Norah. He had eyes for no one else. As for the murder, the thought of it probably never entered his head.

By and by the party broke up, the ladies to dress for their raid on the rue de la Paix, and W.T. and Jerry to return to their hotel.

They parted on excellent terms, W.T. persuading the sisters to dine with him and Jerry the same evening.

The smiling Kathreen escorted the father and son down the passage to the main door of the suite.

'Glad to see you again, sir,' she said, anxious for them to notice her.

The detective beamed at her.

'Thank you, Kathreen. How do you like Paris? Enjoying yourself?'

Kathreen cast her round eyes heaven-ward. 'I am!' she said. 'Since the missus heard about her money we've been going it, I can tell you.'

'Money?' W.T.'s tone was mildly surprised.

The girl raised her eyebrows.

'Haven't you heard? I should have thought you'd be the first to know. The missus has come into all Mr Crowther's money – 'im as was shot.'

10   The Next Move

'Look here, Dad, what are you going to do?' Jerry put the
question aggressively.

The two men were seated together in a deserted corner in the
lounge of their hotel, having just returned from escorting Mrs
Christensen and Norah home after dinner at the Café de Paris.

'What are you going to do?' the boy repeated.

W.T. put his brandy-and-soda down on the glass-topped cane
table, and blinked at his son in mild astonishment.

'Jerry,' he said, 'that Château Yquem has gone to your head –
I should go to bed, my boy.'

Jerry flushed angrily.

'I'm in no mood for that sort of chaff just now,' he said,
without troubling to keep the irritation out of his voice. 'I want
to know what you're doing. Why aren't we going back to England
tomorrow?'

'Because,' said W.T. cheerfully, 'I think we shall do more good
if we stay here.'

'Good?' The boy's voice rose contemptuously. 'I suppose by
that you mean we shall worm out some more disgusting facts
about that murder.'

'Well,' said the detective mildly, 'we did come here for that,
you know.'

Jerry paused for a moment or so before he spoke.

'Anyway,' he said sullenly, 'we didn't come here to take out
girls to dinner and question them. It makes me sick!'

W.T. regarded him solemnly.

'Jerry,' he said at last, 'do you think Norah Bayliss shot Eric
Crowther?'

'Good God, no!'

'Do you think her sister did?'

'N – no, no, of course not.'

'Well, then,' said the old man, leaning back in his chair, 'isn't it the best thing we can do for them to make sure – so that they can never fall under suspicion?'

Jerry frowned and moved uneasily.

'Why, yes – I – I suppose so,' he said at last. 'It's foul about that wretched money.'

W.T. nodded.

'Most extraordinary,' he said. 'Deadwood must be off his head. I ought to have heard of that at once – the girls coming to Paris, too – and not a word from him – I don't know what he's doing over there.'

'Maybe he was relying on your arresting Cellini,' said Jerry.

W.T. frowned. 'Very likely,' he said gloomily. 'Still, he ought to have let me know – especially about the money. I wired for a copy of the will as soon as I got in this afternoon, of course. We shall get it in the morning.'

Jerry sat forward in his chair, clasping his knee.

'She – she *couldn't* have done it,' he said at last.

'Who – Mrs Christensen?'

'Of course.'

W.T. was silent for some moments. 'I don't know,' he said. 'When a woman is goaded beyond all endurance, there's nothing she couldn't do.'

'She *couldn't*,' the boy repeated. 'She couldn't!'

'What makes you think that?'

The old man put the question casually, and the boy answered it with his thought.

'Well – I mean to say – a woman with a sister like that – ' He broke off short before the expression on the old detective's face.

'My dear boy' – W.T. spoke inoffensively – 'that is an argument that may convince you in your present state of blissful lunacy, but you can't expect it to have the same effect on me.'

'Why, d'you think she did it?'

W.T. rumpled his hair, making himself look somehow like a festive owl.

''Pon my soul, Jerry, I don't know,' he said. 'There are times when I could believe anything – I'm going to bed now, anyway.'

He prepared to rise from his chair, but the boy, leaning across the table towards him, kept him seated.

'Dad,' said Jerry, clipping his words in his earnestness; 'that chap Crowther – he deserved to be killed. What does it matter who killed him?'

'What does it matter?' repeated W.T. blankly.

Jerry nodded; his young face became suddenly hard.

'Yes,' he said; 'whoever killed that man did it in self-defence – mental if not physical. Why don't you leave him alone?'

W.T.'s eyes narrowed.

'What do you mean?' he demanded.

'Chuck up the case,' said Jerry. 'Leave it. Don't try to find out any more.'

'Throw up the case!' said the old man, an expression of horror growing on his face. 'Throw up the case? My dear boy, you're mad!'

'I'm not – I feel it would be best, honestly – I feel we ought not to find out any more.'

The old man shook his head.

'Jerry,' he said, 'in our business one must never be afraid to know the truth. You want me to throw up this case – a thing I could never do for my own self-respect's sake – because you're afraid to face what you believe to be true. You believe Mrs Christensen fired that shot – don't interrupt me – I repeat you believe she murdered Eric Crowther, and you're afraid to prove it. That's no good, my boy – a doubt is always dangerous. For her sake as well as for everyone else's we've got to find out all we can. Crowther had some hold over her – some secret which old Estah shared. We've got to find out what that was. We've got to find out why he left a will in her favour: we've got to find out if she is innocent or not.'

Jerry sighed.

'Then you won't give up.'

'Certainly not – I have never heard such a suggestion.' W.T. spoke vigorously and rose to his feet. 'Do you think I'm going to put four or five innocent people under suspicion because in your opinion a suspected woman has a pretty sister? If you weren't in love and therefore insane I should punch your head, my boy.' And the old fellow stalked off to bed.

As for Jerry, he sat there late thinking of Norah.

The morning found W.T. fuming over the English breakfast that a whole army of scandalized French waiters could not have shamed him into forgoing, and when Jerry came down he scowled fiercely at the boy across the table.

'Has it come?' said Jerry, his mind on the will.

'No,' said W.T. 'This'll hold us up another day. They couldn't get hold of it at once, I suppose.'

'Oh, well, you'll get it tonight, no doubt. Anything else?'

'No,' said the detective explosively, 'only a damn silly letter from Deadwood in reply to my report.'

Jerry grinned. He began to see the occasion of his father's irritation. Inspector Deadwood was a well-meaning man who was invariably full of bright suggestions about other people's cases, and no one else on earth had a surer gift of rubbing W.T. up the wrong way.

'Oh!' said Jerry. 'What does he think?'

'He doesn't,' said the detective acidly. 'That's his trouble.'

W.T. shook his head.

'No,' he said; 'it wasn't an accident. The gun didn't suddenly decide to go off on its own. And I don't think a passing monkey did it, nor a man who owed Crowther a grudge in India and happened to be in the Christensens' dining-room at the moment unknown to anyone. I don't think any of these things. This is as clear a case of long-meditated but actually impulsive murder as ever I've seen.'

Jerry nodded.

'You're still determined to go through with it?' he said doubtfully.

'Absolutely,' said W.T. firmly. 'I've never left a case unfinished in my life. The idea of doing such a thing horrifies me. It's my job.'

The boy frowned.

'I can't think why you don't retire,' he said. 'You've got plenty of money – you're not waiting for a pension and you don't like the life. You told old Doc Cave so the other day.' He paused, and then added, as the other did not speak, 'What's the idea of sticking to it like this?'

'There are many parts of my business that are repellent to me, naturally,' said old W.T. sedately, 'but the main thing, the instinct of the chase, is still there. I shall go on grumbling and carrying on until I'm too old.'

Jerry said no more.

Late in the afternoon, the eagerly awaited copy of Eric Crowther's will arrived.

W.T. carried it off to his room immediately, and shut himself up with it. Jerry gave him time to read it, and then went in.

'Any luck?' he said as he closed the door behind him.

W.T. looked up.

'No,' he said. 'Not really – there's one curious thing, though. Listen to this: "All moneys in stock, War Loan, and other securities, besides the balance at my bank, I leave unreservedly to Mrs Roger Christensen of the White Cottage, Brandesdon, Kent, *who ought to have it.*" '

' "Who ought to have it"?' repeated Jerry.

W.T. nodded.

'Now what does that mean – exactly?' he said. 'You see, my boy, we must go into this. If that woman is innocent of the actual murder she must know something about it.'

' "*Who ought to have it* ",' Jerry repeated, the phrase fascinating him. 'Does that mean that she is some – some relative of his?'

W.T. shook his head. 'I don't know. It may, of course, but I hardly think so. Anyway, we shall know before long. Before I left London I put the research department on to Crowther. We shall get a full report of his life, as far as it can be traced, within a day or so. That ought to tell us something. Meanwhile, we must concentrate on Mrs Christensen. You see, there's one rather significant point about this will ...' Jerry glanced up quickly.

'What's that?'

W.T. looked at him.

'The date of it,' he said. 'It was made six years ago.'

Jerry caught his breath.

'What's our next move, then?'

W.T. glanced at his watch.

'The night train for Marseilles and the Mediterranean coast starts at seven o'clock from the Gare de Lyon,' he said. 'We must catch it. They're only twelve hours ahead of us.'

Jerry sighed and began to pack his bag in silence. Life was beginning to present problems more difficult than he had ever dreamed possible.

They caught the train without fuss.

It was still early autumn, and the Mediterranean 'season' had not yet begun, so there were comparatively few travellers on the train, and father and son secured a compartment to themselves.

Jerry was very silent, however; the situation did not appeal to him. For the last twenty-four hours at least Norah had filled up his horizon, and all else seemed comparatively small and insignificant.

W.T. sat in his corner, his 'pillow' behind his head and his arms folded upon his breast.

Gradually the long night wore away and the morning brought a new country of olive trees and red soil, and at last the great black rock jutting up against sea and sky as they came into Marseilles.

The rest of the journey along the coast to Mentone interested Jerry in spite of himself. The fairy-story mountains with castles a-top on one side, and the everlasting succession of incredibly blue bays on the other, appealed to him irresistibly. It was hot, too, by the time they reached the railway station at Mentone.

They chose a quiet hotel in the busier and unfashionable quarter of the town.

It was Jerry's first visit to the south coast, and the gaiety and colour of the scene enchanted him. The crazy carrier's carts from the mountains, with their noisy, villainous-looking drivers, the girls with their marvellous coiffures, the brightness everywhere – it was all new and delightful.

They were walking down one of the narrow streets, the

jabbering throng pressing about them, when W.T. suddenly touched his son's arm.

'Who's that?' he murmured.

Jerry followed the direction of his father's glance and saw a man seated at one of the many little tables upon the pavement outside a café.

His blue suit was very new, and fitted his meagre form abominably, his bright brown shoes swung a good two inches off the ground, and his pale-grey hat was set well on the back of his bony head. Jerry stared at him.

The clothes were different, of course, but there was something familiar about those red-rimmed eyes and that revoltingly sticky-looking, yellow-grey moustache.

'Good Lord!' he murmured. 'Clarry Gale!'

W.T. nodded, and taking the boy's arm, led him gently in the opposite direction.

'Don't look back,' he said. 'I don't want him to see us. Now what in blazes is *he* doing here?'

11　The Record

'No, Jerry, my boy, I think our best plan is still to lie low until we get that record from home. We want all the information we can get before we interview anyone.'

Old W.T. sat back in a chair on the balcony outside his bedroom window in the hotel, and puffed his cigarette thoughtfully as he spoke. They had been in Mentone two days now, without making much progress.

It was a typical southern night, the air warm, and noisy with the far-off buzz of the town. The sky was fretted with stars, and not a breath of wind stirred the scalloped frills of the striped awnings over the café windows. The old man's voice sounded soft and deep in the semi-darkness.

Jerry stirred.

'Well, we know where they are,' he remarked.

W.T. nodded.

'That's something done, anyway,' he said. 'But now we must wait for the record. That phrase "who ought to have it" worries me.'

'Clarry Gale, too,' said Jerry slowly. 'He seems to have come into money. One curious thing about Crowther's murder is the sudden wealth of the folk who were associated with him.'

'I thought that.' W.T. stirred, and his chair creaked in the darkness. 'Gale wasn't mentioned in the will, though,' he went on after a pause. 'No, you bet your life, Jerry, if he's come into money it is through his own dishonest endeavour. The sight of him astounded me. It must have something to do with the two girls being here, of course.'

'Why?'

'Well' – W.T.'s tone was expressive – 'a man like Clarry

Gale doesn't come to Mentone for fun. He might possibly go to Blackpool. I believe he'd go to Monte Carlo without a motive, but Mentone – never!'

'But what could he have to do with Mrs Christensen and Norah? Do you suggest he's employed by them?' Jerry put the question aggressively.

W.T. raised his eyebrows.

'That hadn't occurred to me,' he said, 'and it doesn't seem likely, for I don't see what he could be doing for them; but he might be employed by someone else to watch them. I don't know enough yet to judge of that.'

There was silence for some moments then Jerry spoke:

'Of course,' he said, 'we don't know yet what hold Crowther had over Gale, do we?'

'No, not exactly,' the detective admitted, 'but I think I've a a pretty shrewd idea. I sent for the report of the last case he was in.'

'Oh?' Jerry spoke with new interest. 'What was that?'

W.T. lit another cigarette before he replied.

'A burglary, you know,' he said. 'A rather nasty affair – several people were implicated. A man called Grant had a house in Feering Park Crescent, W., where he lived alone with his two servants, a man called Briggs and a cook, a Mrs Phail. One night a gang broke in on them – Gale, Abrahams and Goody. Grant slept in the front of the house and heard nothing, but Briggs and Mrs Phail, who had rooms over the kitchens, were awakened. Briggs crept downstairs and surprised the three. Abrahams made a bolt for it with Briggs after him. The other two climbed out of a side window, Goody first, right into the arms of a waiting constable. When they went back to the house, it was found that Mrs Phail, hurrying down the kitchen stairs after Briggs, had slipped and, falling, cut her head open on a zinc bath standing at the foot of them. She was dead. There was a theory at the time that her fall was not entirely due to accident, and there was a lot of talk, but no one could prove anything and the three got off with stiff sentences.' He paused.

'Well?' said Jerry.

'Well, don't you see,' said the detective, 'Gale was the last to leave the house, and supposing the theorists to have been correct, Gale was the man to have done the punching, because neither of the other two was the type to be silent for a pal's sake if his own skin was in danger.'

'Then you say Gale killed the woman?' began Jerry.

W.T. made a deprecating gesture.

'My dear boy, I don't say anything, I only *think* that he may possibly have done so. You see, the only plausible explanation to my mind of his ten years of uncongenial work with Crowther is that he was virtually in prison. Now, the only other thing besides bars that would keep Clarry Gale in prison is a fear of his precious neck ... I mean to say,' he went on, 'supposing Crowther *knew* that Gale had killed the woman – suppose he could prove it – and being the curious mental type we know he was, preferred to keep Gale under his thumb rather than give him up to the police. That would explain that ten years, wouldn't it?'

'It would,' said Jerry. 'Of course it would. But how could Crowther get to know of the crime?'

'That,' admitted W.T., 'is the chink in the armour.'

'Chink?' said Jerry, grinning. 'It's a darn big hole.'

W.T. nodded.

'Perhaps you're right. Perhaps you're right,' he said affably. 'But I've got a sort of feeling that that is more or less what happened. I don't know how – yet. But I think you'll find that I'm right. I've got that impression.'

'As you had about Cellini?' put in Jerry.

W.T. coughed.

'That, Jerry, is unfilial,' he said sedately.

Their conversation was abruptly ended by a tapping on the door. Jerry went to open it and came back with a package.

'It's come,' he said.

'It's from headquarters.' The old detective opened the long envelope, and taking the typed manuscript from within, spread it out upon a table under the light. Jerry leant over his shoulder, and they read it together.

'Good heavens!'

W.T. laughed shortly with pure excitement. 'Listen to this,' he said, '. . . *lived for some time in a house in Feering Park Crescent, W., under the name of Grant.*'

'My God!' said Jerry. 'That means – '

'That we weren't so far off the tack as you thought,' said the old man. 'Now, let me see, how does this go on? Oh yes – *frequent visits to Paris, believed to be on the business of research work connected with the brain.* Then a great deal that we know. *Settled down in Brandesdon, Kent, with Italian secretary.* Yes, yes . . . yes. There's nothing else much there.'

W.T. ran his eye down the page. 'Oh no; wait a moment. What's this?' he added, and read aloud:

The main bulk of his property was derived from his ward, Jack Grey, killed in France, 1914, at the age of twenty. As far as can be ascertained, Grey was placed under Crowther's guardianship two years before and lived with him for a short period in Brandesdon, Kent. At Grey's death his estate passed automatically to Crowther.

W.T. put down the manuscript and looked at his son.

'At last,' he said slowly.

Jerry looked puzzled. 'I'm afraid I don't follow quite,' he said. 'Who was this Jack Grey?'

W.T. smiled.

'That's just what we've got to find out, my boy,' he said, 'but the fact that he existed at all tells us something. It was his money, you see.'

'What money?' said Jerry.

'Why, the money that Mrs Christensen "ought to have", of course.'

Jerry sat down on the bed and rubbed his fingers through his sleek hair.

'Who d'you *think* this fellow Grey was?' he said. 'Some relative?'

The detective did not answer for a moment. He sat down in an armchair and leant back.

'He may have been, of course,' he said at last. 'We must find that out. But there are many other alternatives. He may have left a will that Crowther suppressed, or expressed a wish that Crowther disregarded. We don't *know* anything about him yet. Everything we say is bound to be conjecture until we get some more facts. There may be nothing of importance in it after all, but there is one rather significant point in that report.'

Jerry crossed over to the table and looked down at it.

'Oh,' he said, 'what's that?'

W.T. closed his eyes and spoke slowly, trying to remember the actual wording of the phrase.

'Doesn't it say "Jack Grey lived with Crowther at Brandesdon"?'

'Yes,' said Jerry. '"Lived with him for a short period in Brandesdon, Kent".'

The detective nodded.

'I thought so,' he said. 'Doesn't it strike you as curious, Jerry, that no one mentioned him to us when we were making inquiries about Crowther? Surely the women would remember him ... a lad about twenty, killed in France?'

Jerry grimaced.

'I don't know,' he said; 'it's some time ago ... people do forget.'

'Yes, but not when they're asked point-blank,' the detective persisted. 'When I asked Mrs Christensen on the morning of the inquest if in her recollection Crowther had ever had any visitors, she insisted that he had not in all the six years and odd months he had lived at the "Dene". Why didn't she remember Grey?'

The boy did not answer, but sat staring fixedly at the toes of his shoes.

'As for Gale,' W.T. continued suddenly, 'the fact that Crowther actually *was* the Grant in the Feering Park Crescent case is most enlightening. I think I must have been nearly exactly right in my guess there. What an amazing mentality the dead man must have had!'

As Jerry rose to his feet, an oblique-eyed boots boy appeared in the doorway.

'Gentleman downstair' weesh to speak wid monsieur,' he said.

'Oh,' said W.T. 'What name?'

'Meester Clarrigale.'

'Clarry Gale!' W.T. and Jerry exchanged glances, and the detective spoke.

'Show him up here, will you?' – and added as the door closed: 'We're in luck tonight, Jerry.'

12   The Happy Thought of Mr Gale

'Well, guv'nor, 'ow *are* yer?' Mr Gale paused in the doorway, his hat in his hand and his peculiarly unpleasant little rat face clothed in a smile of apparently genuine pleasure.

''Ow *are* yer?' he repeated with exaggerated cordiality, and as the father and son sat silent, looking at him unsmilingly, he closed the door behind him, and sneaking further into the room, perched himself on the edge of a chair, his knees wide apart and his heels touching some two inches off the ground.

He continued to beam, and again Jerry was struck by the weakness in his unpleasant face.

W.T. sat looking at him, his bright eyes hard and very penetrating under their white brows. Clarry Gale continued to grin, however, not in the least discomposed by his somewhat cold reception. He looked round the room approvingly.

'Nice an' comfortable 'ere, looks like,' he remarked after a pause.

Still W.T. did not speak, and the man's uncertain gaze travelled to the window through which the lights of the town were just visible from where he sat.

'*Strik*-ingly beautiful place this,' he went on in the ludicrous conversational tone he had adopted. '*Strik-ingly* beautiful – the Coat Daz Ure.' And he sniffed vigorously.

The detective flicked his cigarette ash and then looked across at the unattractive object on the chair that was so much too high for him.

'Well,' he said at last, 'what's the game, Gale?'

'Gime – wot gime?' Mr Gale's expression was innocent.

W.T. smiled faintly.

'To what am I indebted for this visit?' he said gravely.

Clarry Gale wriggled on his uncomfortable chair.

'You mean w'y 'ave I come?'

'Exactly.'

Mr Gale sniffed again, and Jerry noticed how long and damp his moustaches were – like a drayhorse's, he reflected.

'W'y 'ave I come?' Mr Gale repeated, with jovial indignation. 'W'y 'ave I come? You're a nice one, you are – is that the w'y to welcome an old friend in a foreign land?'

Jerry began to wax impatient. The man annoyed him, and his arms ached to chuck him out. W.T. appeared to be getting a certain amount of amusement out of the interview, however, and his eyes twinkled when next he spoke.

'I beg your pardon, Gale,' he said; 'I did not understand at first – you have just come on a friendly visit?'

'Yes, that's right,' said Mr Gale, his grin returning. 'Jus' a frien'ly visit – like anyone might pay.'

'Like anyone might pay,' repeated W.T. with satisfaction, and there was silence in the room.

Mr Gale cleared his throat encouragingly once or twice, but neither W.T. nor Jerry seemed anxious to take the hint, and after a while he was forced to reopen the conversation himself.

'Down 'ere on business?' he inquired at last with exaggerated casualness.

'Sure,' said the detective, and again there was silence.

Mr Gale's feet began to swing to and fro and his eyes wandered vainly round the room for a topic of conversation. W.T. came to his rescue.

'Are you on business, Gale?'

'Me?' The little man shot a suspicious glance at the detective, but the old man's face was serene and benevolent as ever. 'Well,' he continued at last, spreading the word out until it was an explanation in itself, 'in a way yes, and in a way no, as *you* might say. Mainly I'm 'ere on a holiday – '

'Oh yes?' said W.T. with innocent interest.

Gale eyed the other man doubtfully.

'My 'ealth wasn't so good, yer see, an' my doctor 'e said to me, "The Souf of France is the place for you, my boy." So, 'appening to 'ave a bit of money left me sudden by a frien', I comes over 'ere.'

'For your health's sake?' said W.T.

'Well, w'y not?' said Mr Gale.

'Why not?' said the detective blandly. 'Ten years' hard isn't good for anyone's health.'

'Eh?' Mr Gale looked up sharply. 'Wot yer drivin' at?'

'Driving at? Nothing. What should I be driving at?'

'I don't know.' Mr Gale shifted uneasily in his chair. 'We're all matey 'ere, aren't we?'

'I think so.'

'Wot d'you mean – "think so"? We are, ain't we? I'm just payin' you a friendly visit because I 'appened to know you was down 'ere – that's all, ain't it?'

'That's all,' said W.T., adding innocently, 'as far as I know.'

'Then 'oo's talking about ten years' hard?' said Mr Gale, to whose ears the words had had an ominous sound.

'That was only a figure of speech,' said the detective easily. 'I was referring to your life at the "Dene", Brandesdon. That was pretty hard, wasn't it?'

'It was 'ell,' said Mr Gale explicitly. ''E was a one, 'e was – orf 'is bloomin' onion, I believe. They oughter 'ave 'ad 'is 'ead up at the 'orsepitals to 'ave a look in after 'e was dead. I didn't 'arf lead a life wiv 'im.'

'I wonder you stuck it.' W.T. put the question casually, and Clarry Gale nearly fell for it. His expression changed, and he opened his mouth to speak, but caught himself up in time and shrugged his shoulders elaborately to hide his sudden reticence.

'Jobs are hard to get, guv'nor,' he said, adopting a pious whine. 'Especially when you've been the type of man wot I 'ave,' he added sententiously.

'Eh?' said W.T.

Clarry Gale nodded virtuously.

'I said wot I *ave* been,' he repeated pointedly. 'I mean, we're all frien's 'ere. You know wot I 'ave been – it's no good me pretendin' wiv' you.'

'Not in the least,' said W.T. with polite ambiguousness.

'That's right, then,' said Mr Gale happily. 'But bein' down 'ere for a noliday, and seein' an old frien' in a bit of a fix as you might say, I thought I'd come along and give you a 'and, see?'

W.T.'s expression did not change.

'That's very nice of you, Gale,' he said pleasantly. 'But what makes you think I'm in a bit of a fix, as you call it?'

Clarry Gale grinned and winked knowingly.

'You can't come it over me, guv'nor,' he said. 'I know the police so well – one way an' another. Still, wot is there to be touchy over? It ain't everyone who can find 'is way about a foreign town all in a minute. You've jest been unlucky, that's all. But it so 'appens that I'm in a persition to give you just the bit of information you require.'

W.T. still smiled, but there was a faintly mystified expression in the back of his eyes.

'Turning detective in your old age, Gale?' he said. 'How d'you like the job?'

'Suits me fine. Now, guv'nor, what's it worth to you?'

A light of understanding flashed into W.T.'s face.

'What is what worth?' he demanded.

Clarry Gale shook his head.

'Play fair, guv'nor, play fair,' he admonished. 'Plain speaking asks for plain speaking, don't it?'

'It does,' agreed W.T. 'What is this piece of information you want to sell me?'

Gale looked doubtful.

'You never was a man to act dirty, guv'nor,' he said. 'Wot yer playin' at? You know you've been 'anging around 'ere these last two days lookin' for somebody you ain't been able to lay your 'ands on.'

'Oh,' said W.T., who was beginning to see how the land lay. 'And what makes you think I haven't been able to find – er – what I've been looking for?'

'Well, you ain't 'ad no interview, 'ave you?' The words broke from the old lag involuntarily, and W.T. glanced at him sharply.

'How do you know I want to have an interview?' he demanded.

Clarry Gale looked blank.

'Wot's the idea of coming down 'ere, then?' he said. 'I know
wot you're after – I ain't barmy – I just thought I could give you
a little 'elp, that's all. You see, I 'appen to know where they are.'

'They – who are they?'

Mr Gale leant back as well as he could in the high chair,
tucked his hands in his trouser pockets and attempted to look
disgusted.

'Now, that's coming it a bit too thick – a bit too thick, that is,'
he commented. 'You know 'oo I mean.'

W.T. crossed one knee over the other and folded his arms.

'Gale,' he said slowly, 'when you saw me here, did it never
occur to you that I might be interested in *you*?'

'*Me?*' Mr Gale's mouth dropped open and his little ferrety
eyes grew wide. 'Me?' he repeated. 'You're jokin', guv'nor ...
You ain't got nothin' against me. I've gone honest for ten years,
I 'ave.'

The detective did not speak, and Mr Gale's spirits returned.

'My alibi was all right too, wasn't it?' he said.

'Oh, quite,' said W.T. mildly.

'Well, then, w'y the 'okey-pokey?' Mr Gale was aggrieved.
'Let's get down to business. I can give you the hotel of them two
girls, number of their suite an' everything. Wot's it worth?'

W.T. hesitated.

'I'll give you two hundred-franc notes for it,' he said at last.

'Two perishin' quid? That ain't much. If I'd ha' thought that
was all you could rise to, guv'nor, I wouldn't 'a' troubled to 'a'
come.'

The old detective shrugged his shoulders, and taking out his
note-case selected the two notes he had mentioned.

'Take it or leave it,' he said.

Gale took the money, still grumbling.

'If you wasn't an old frien' things would be different, I can tell
you,' he said, 'but in mem'ry of the parst an' one thing an'
another 'ere you are.' He put his hand in his pocket and drawing

out an envelope thrust it into the detective's face. W.T. glanced at it and put it in his note-case.

Gale edged towards the door. 'I'll be goin', then,' he said. 'Glad to 'ave seen you again and to 'ave done what I could for you. Any other time you want me, I'm staying down the road in the "Maison Sud".'

'For long?'

'No – o'ny a d'y or so. So long, guv'nor. So long to you too, sir.' And Clarry Gale pattered out.

Jerry looked at his father, who was still seated, his arms folded.

'What's the idea of paying for a piece of information we already have?'

W.T. took out the envelope Gale had given him.

'Norah Bayliss and Grace Christensen. Suite Number nine. Hôtel Magnifique,' he read aloud.

'Well, we know that already,' said Jerry. 'At least, we know the hotel; the number of the suite isn't necessary.'

W.T. nodded absently. He was grave now, and his eyes were veiled with their heavy lids.

'I don't see what you were driving at,' Jerry persisted. 'Why didn't you let me pitch the grinning little hypocrite into the street?'

'Jerry, my boy,' W.T. spoke mildly. 'You haven't the mind of a detective. Gale has given us some very interesting information. Don't grudge him his francs.'

'The number of a hotel suite – ' began Jerry contemptuously.

'Quite,' said W.T., 'just think of the things Gale has told us. Unintentionally perhaps, but still told us – facts that are of great interest to us.'

'I don't see,' said Jerry.

W.T. sat up in his chair and ticked the points off on his fingers as he spoke.

'First of all,' he said easily, 'he has told us that he is watching us. Secondly, that he is watching Mrs Christensen and Norah – probably he followed them out here. Thirdly, he is in touch with them – on speaking terms, but not in their employ – '

'Hold a moment,' cut in Jerry. 'I don't see how you make that out.'

W.T. looked at him gravely.

'He must be on speaking terms with them to know that we have not had an interview with Mrs Christensen yet, but, on the other hand, he can't be in their employ, or he would not come to us to sell us information that would mean him losing his job ... I'm afraid it's blackmail. He knows something.'

'Blackmail? Gale blackmailing Mrs Christensen?' Jerry spoke quickly. 'That's impossible, Dad – I mean, your own argument cuts both ways. Gale wouldn't come to us to sell us information that would – would mean you getting at Mrs Christensen and so removing his source of money.'

W.T. nodded. 'That's true,' he said; 'but, you see, Gale knew that I was bound to find Mrs Christensen sooner or later – he wanted to know how much I knew, and also to make sure that I wasn't after *him*. Incidentally he thought he might pick up anything there was going before the smash. I know that type so well. They don't think ahead at all. Probably he guessed I had seen him, and wondered why I was so quiet – folk with uneasy consciences get nerves, Jerry.'

'Blackmail,' repeated the boy, to whom the idea was new, and horrible for its very likelihood. 'If Mrs Christensen is paying Gale blackmail it's pretty certain that she – she's guilty – and Norah ... Oh, my God, Dad!'

Old W.T. looked across at the boy's drawn face and his own expression softened.

'The next move,' he said, 'is mine.'

13   Mrs Christensen's Secret

As W.T. walked down the steep, narrow streets of the old border village no one would have dreamed that he was a detective on a case of murder.

He looked upon the scene around him with mild interest. His face was already tanned by the intense sun, and it looked dark against the whiteness of his hair. It was early yet, and the town was alive and busy, its inhabitants hard at work before the mid-day sun should make energetic labour an impossibility, but already the stony shore was gay with bathers. The warm waters of the bay were exquisitely blue – more blue, it seemed, than the sky, and so clear that from the road the detective could see the shadows of the shoals of little fish in its shallow depths. Every hour sleek cars and strange old canopied victorias from the station brought new arrivals to this coast of pleasure.

As W.T. passed by several faces in the crowds recognized him, and on these occasions the man or woman would glance at him sharply and move on hurriedly. These were society crooks – pick-pockets and confidence men, girl decoys and cardsharpers, come to the South from every corner of the Continent. They would work all along the coast, drifting from Mentone to Monte Carlo, from Monte Carlo to Cannes and Nice as the season progressed and their whims advised them.

W.T. was not looking forward to his task that morning; he stalked on towards the hotel with his face grave and his expression determined.

The Hôtel Magnifique stands at the far end of the road that runs round the bay – hardly five hundred yards from the Italian border. It is a huge, flat building facing the sea, a projecting wing at either end of the main block. In the courtyard thus formed there is a garden, semi-tropical and very formal, but pleasant enough for a country in which there seem to be no birds in the trees and no freshness in the leaves.

As the detective turned into this garden he saw her.

Grace Christensen was a woman of the pretty, graceful, feminine type that is not too clever. Just now she was seated in the shadow of the banana tree outside the hotel porch. W.T. noticed a subtle change in her bearing since he had last seen her in Paris. She was paler, and although her attention was fixed upon the paper on her knee and he could not see her eyes, the detective knew by the way her fingers tore nervously at the gloves in her lap that she was afraid.

'Mrs Christensen,' he said.

At the sound of his voice a little stifled scream escaped the woman, and she looked up at him, every tinge of colour vanishing from her face.

The detective was astonished. Either Mrs Christensen had been a marvellous actress in Paris and was now taken completely by surprise, or in Paris she had thought herself safe and now had reason to believe that her guilt had been discovered. In W.T.'s private opinion most women, while being strictly moral according to their own codes, very often had no sense of the law at all.

'Mr Challoner?' she said, and her voice wavered. 'Why have you come here?'

'Suppose we walk down there,' he suggested, indicating the hill road into Italy. 'I want to talk to you.'

The woman rose to her feet, and stood hesitating, her face ashy and her slender body swaying a little.

'I – I don't think I can walk,' she said at last, 'but we have a sitting-room here – Norah is out – we shouldn't be disturbed.'

W.T. followed her into the great dim hotel that was so oddly reminiscent of the Victoria and Albert Museum, and within five minutes found himself seated opposite her in the pink-and-gold monstrosity of a lounge in suite No. 9.

In that five minutes she seemed to have become old. Lines had appeared round her mouth and under her wide, deep-blue eyes. The woman was the first to speak.

'Well?' she said softly. 'Tell me, why have you come?' There was a certain determined bravery in her tone.

'I want to talk to you,' he said cautiously. 'There are certain things about Eric Crowther that I want to know.'

The woman shot a terrified glance at him.

'I told you all I knew on the day he died,' she said.

W.T. shook his head.

'Let us be honest with each other,' he said. 'The situation is difficult, and – '

'Oh, it *is*!' The words seemed to be wrung from her heart, and he paused and looked at her in surprise. Neither the words nor her tone seemed to suggest guilt. There was fear there certainly, but not admission. 'I – I'm sorry; I ought not to have interrupted you,' she went on. 'I will tell you all I know.'

'Everything?' The detective looked at her keenly as he spoke. 'I assure you it will be the best thing you can do, the more one knows the more fairly one can judge.'

The woman nodded.

'I will tell you everything,' she repeated.

'Good,' said the detective. 'Then suppose we start at the beginning. Who was Jack Grey?'

W.T.'s tone was casual, but had he bellowed the name loud enough for all the world to hear the effect upon the woman could not have been more extraordinary. She sprang from her chair and shrank away from him, her face frozen into a mask in which only the eyes seemed to be alive.

'Oh, my God! – my God!' she whispered.

'Tell me,' he said, 'nothing matters now but the truth.'

'Oh, again – *again!*' The words broke from the girl in an agony of weariness. 'I thought that was over for ever. Must I have it again – always, always that? Is there never any peace?'

W.T. leant forward, his face grave and his eyes troubled.

'Can't you explain all this, Mrs Christensen? Don't you see if you don't speak I must draw my own conclusions from the words you let fall, and I may so easily be wrong.'

'Mr Challoner,' she said, 'you – you detectives can – can keep things secret if you want to, can't you? I – I mean,' she went on hurriedly, 'if a thing that happened a long time ago wasn't anything to do really with – with the crime you were investigating, it wouldn't all have to come out, would it? – not if it wouldn't help and would just spoil people's lives – *young* lives?'

W.T. stared at her, his mind busy knitting together the loose threads she had given him, and suddenly the truth dawned upon him.

'Mrs Christensen,' he said, 'your child – is not your husband's. Jack Grey was . . .'

'My lover.' The two words broke from the woman in a whisper, and she bowed her head over her hands.

W.T. sat silent, the situation becoming more and more clear to him at every moment.

'I see,' he said.

'Your husband does not know?'

She shook her head. 'No – *must* he know now? Must it all come out at last?' She was becoming hysterical again, and the old man spoke reassuringly.

'I will do everything in my power to prevent it,' he said. 'If you tell me everything I feel sure that that can be arranged.'

'You promise?'

'I promise.'

The woman fixed her eyes on his face.

'It was wrong but it was understandable,' she began softly, 'and if it hadn't been for that fiend Crowther no one would ever have known. You – you see, Jack and I were sweethearts from childhood – we lived near each other, and when we grew up we fell in love . . .' She paused, and in at the windows the heat-laden breeze brought the laughter and perfume of the fashionable throng without.

'His father died just after he left school,' she went on. 'The old man was an eccentric, a great student of the brain, and he admired Crowther's work – he was wonderfully clever, you know. Old Professor Grey had no one to appoint as guardian over Jack, and when he knew he was dying he wrote to Crowther and asked him as a fellow-scientist if he would undertake the charge. To everyone's astonishment Crowther said he would.'

Again she was silent, and W.T. nodded encouragingly.

'Crowther opposed our marriage from the start,' she went on, her voice very small and ineffably sad in the sunlit room. 'We were so much in love and so very young. We were very helpless too. Before the war parents and guardians had more power than they have today.' She sighed, and the detective wondered that she could find this so real and so sad when there was a noose hanging over her head; the murder was an unimportant factor in her mind.

'So he parted us,' she said suddenly. 'He was a curious man, Mr Challoner. He seemed – seemed to enjoy doing it, as if he knew how he was hurting us, and liked doing it.'

W.T. nodded comprehendingly and the woman went on:

'I was heart-broken,' she said simply. 'I felt as if my world had come to an end, as if all the goodness had gone out of life. I was unhappy at home, nothing seemed to matter. Then Roger came along. He proposed to me and I married him. He was strong then, you know, and very handsome. He was very kind to me.' Again her voice died away, and the detective began to see the pitiful little story in its entirety.

'That was just over six years ago?' he said.

She nodded. 'Nearer seven. We went to live in Brandesdon at the White Cottage. I had made up my mind to forget Jack entirely – I wanted to make Roger a good wife – he had been so kind to me – and then – he found me.'

'Who? Jack?'

She shook her head.

'No. I don't believe Jack would have done it. I mean Crowther.' An expression of utter loathing came into her eyes, and again the detective marvelled that she should give herself away so frankly. 'Crowther took the "Dene" because we had the White Cottage,' she said. 'You may think me mad for saying so, but I'm sure of it ... He was like that – amazingly clever in some things, amazingly small and cruel in others. He came to live there, and brought Jack with him. That was at the beginning of the war.'

There was silence in the room, and the detective, divining something of what she felt, did not speak.

'We held out for a long time,' she said at last. 'We were very good. Crowther used to watch us – used to hint things to Roger, but he believed in me – that is what made me true to him, I think ... until ...' She paused, and then began to speak again in a low emotional whisper – rocking herself backwards and forwards in her chair the while as though to soothe her nerves and keep herself from crying. 'It was the last time I ever saw him,' she began. 'Roger had gone with his regiment to the front the day before, and I was alone in the house save for Estah, and suddenly I saw Jack coming down the path. He was going to France the next day and had come to say good-bye.'

She began to cry softly to herself.

'I can't tell you what happened,' she said, looking up suddenly. 'I just knew I loved him and didn't care about anything save that he was going away. We just belonged to each other, no one else mattered.' Again she was silent, and the detective let her remain so until she chose to speak again.

'The next morning,' she said at last, 'he went back to the "Dene", and before he left he made Crowther swear to look after me whatever happened to him ... He didn't realize what he was *telling* Crowther. Then he went away. I never saw him again. Three days after he landed he was shot.'

W.T.'s expression was kind.

'And then?' he said gently.

'Then,' she said, so quietly that he hardly heard her, 'then Roger came back – crippled, as you see him. He felt it terribly. He had always been so strong, so keen on riding and games. I think he would have died if it hadn't been for the baby – he was so proud of it – so glad because of it. I – I couldn't tell him, could I? – could I?'

W.T. shook his head.

'Are you fond of your husband?'

'I adore him,' she said simply. 'You don't know how wonderful he is – how patient – how kind to me. I didn't realize it until he came back wounded. But, you see, since then my life has been a hell – Crowther *knew*.'

The old man rose to his feet and strode down the room. The

story was clear to him now, and he could not help but be moved by it.

'He knew,' he repeated. 'He held it over you?'

'Always! ... Never any rest day or night. He used to frighten me until I was hysterical with terror, and then gloat over me. Oh, how I longed and prayed that I might die! But even of that I was afraid. What chance would my poor baby have with a man of that type knowing the secret of her birth? As long as I was alive Crowther would satisfy himself tormenting me.'

W.T. rumpled his hair.

From his point of view the most terrible part of the story was that it looped the rope round the woman's own neck – it supplied her with a good and sufficient motive for the crime – just such a motive that a jury would understand.

The woman's next remark startled him considerably.

'Oh,' she said involuntarily, with heart-felt relief in her tone, 'I *was* glad to know that he was dead.'

'My dear lady – ' he began.

'Oh, you don't understand,' she said swiftly. 'He made life a nightmare for the whole household. He maddened everyone – '

'Estah knew, of course?' said W.T., the recollection of the old woman's attitude coming back suddenly to his mind.

'Oh yes – of course.'

'And Norah?'

At the mention of her sister's name the woman stiffened perceptibly, and W.T. was conscious of a new barrier of reserve put up against him.

'No,' she said stiffly, and was silent.

W.T. was perplexed. Was there some new secret? And why was the woman not terror-stricken now? She was on guard – defensive. But since his assurance that her secret should not come out she seemed almost calm, not like a woman in fear of her life.

'Crowther was cheated of one thing,' she said, and there was a suspicion of a smile round her mouth. 'When Jack was killed he told me that he had made a will in my favour, but that if ever it was proved, suspicion would fall upon me and my baby; but he didn't make it clear enough – no one noticed it.'

'"*Who ought to have it?*"' said W.T.

Mrs Christensen looked at him sharply.

'Yes, that was it,' she said. 'How did you know?'

W.T. did not reply, but his eyes were troubled.

'Mrs Christensen,' he said at last, 'why were you so upset to see me this morning?'

The woman shook her head nervously.

'I – I wasn't. I was surprised to see you – that was all.'

'That is not true,' said W.T. gently. 'We agreed to play fair, didn't we? You have been frank and helpful, but now you are hiding something. Why were you afraid to see me?'

'I was not – just surprised.'

W.T. sighed and tried another tack.

'By the way,' he said casually, but watching her narrowly at the same time, 'have you seen anything of Clarry Gale?'

Mrs Christensen raised her eyebrows.

'I've never heard of him,' she said.

W.T.'s eyes narrowed. 'He sometimes calls himself William Lacy.'

'Oh!' The shaft had gone home. The woman sat up stiffly in her chair, every muscle taut, and her eyes frightened.

'No,' she said, and her tone showed her a poor actress.

W.T. frowned.

'Did you know he was in Mentone?'

'No.' Again there was no surprise in her tone: nothing but defiance.

W.T. was puzzled. If the woman couldn't act she was certainly not behaving as if she was guilty. She was hiding something, and she was apprehensive; but there was something missing.

Yet she must have done it, he told himself. The evidence was all against her now. The motive was there – the opportunity was there, and yet ... yet why, if she shot Crowther, did she go out of the french windows again, allowing Cellini to come in and rob the body before she dashed back through the room to give the alarm?

W.T. looked at her as she sat there, her head held high, her eyes scared like a colt's, and he wondered.

'Mrs Christensen,' he said pleadingly, 'won't you tell me all you know?'

'I have – what more *can* I tell you?'

'Who shot Crowther?'

'I don't know.' Again he was struck by her curious inability to lie. She *did* know, then . . .

'Did *you*?' W.T. put the question slowly.

'I? Of course not.' There was no fear in her tone, no surprise. She laughed at him naturally.

W.T. marvelled at her, and he was mystified too. The end of the puzzle was not yet.

'Mrs Christensen,' he said gently, 'I must ask you not to leave this town without communicating with me . . . this is only a precautionary matter, you understand?'

'Oh, quite,' she said, in a tone that told him that she did not. 'Mr Challoner – you remember your promise – my secret?'

He looked at her vaguely, his mind on the crime.

'My baby,' she said helplessly. 'You promised.'

'I will keep my word,' he assured her gravely.

As he went off down the stairs he marvelled. 'No sense of proportion,' he said. 'None at all . . . Now, I wonder . . .'

14 The Blackmailer

When W.T. walked back to his hotel from his interview with Mrs Christensen, the sun was high in the sky and the heat poured down upon the narrow deserted streets like a scourge. The detective strode on quickly without noticing it, however, his eyes fixed straight ahead of him and his forehead wrinkled with perplexity.

Had Mrs Christensen been the only person in the White Cottage at the time of the murder who had had both a motive for and an opportunity to kill Crowther, there could have been now no doubt in his mind of her guilt; but she had not been so by any means. There was circumstantial evidence strong enough to arrest almost anyone in the household, but of actual proof there was none.

The Cellini affair had not been pleasant to report, and for his pride's sake he was not anxious to repeat the experience. Subconsciously, also, he was loth to believe her a murderess. If she was, her behaviour contradicted all his theories. What puzzled him more than anything else, was the fact that she seemed to know – or to think she knew – the real offender.

'No,' he said at last under his breath. 'No, she must have been acting – trying to throw me off the scent – she must be guilty.'

He was in no enviable frame of mind when he at last entered the hotel looking for Jerry. There was no sign of the boy, and he was just about to stride off up to his room when his eyes fell upon a girl seated by a window looking on to the street. It was Norah

At the moment that he caught sight of her she turned, saw him sprang to her feet and came hurrying across the room.

'Oh, Mr Challoner,' she said thankfully, 'I am glad to see you I'm so scared about Jerry.'

'About Jerry? Where's Jerry?'

'That's it,' said the girl. 'I don't know. You see, I came to him and told him something about that awful man Lacy, and he just sort of went mad – he said, "Wait here till I come back," and dashed out of the hotel. That was two hours ago.'

W.T. looked down at the girl, a slightly dazed expression in his eyes.

'Let's sit down,' he said. 'And then suppose you tell me all about it.'

The girl nodded eagerly and seated herself opposite him at a table in a deserted corner of the room.

Norah was clearly anxious to talk about Jerry, and the old detective realized that she was in love with the boy.

'Well, you see,' the girl began, 'I was worried, so I came to Jerry.'

'Just the person!' commented W.T. acidly to himself, while outwardly he smiled and nodded. A moment later, however, he was frowning.

'You *came* to him?' he said. 'How did you know where he was?'

The girl sighed.

'I'll tell you all about it if you'll only listen,' she said. 'You see, it all happened like this. Ever since we've been down here we've been worried by that awful valet person of Mr Crowther's – William Lacy. He called on us the first day we arrived, and wanted to see my sister alone. I wanted to send him away, but Grace said she'd see him. She did, and since then he's always coming. I can't get rid of him. Grace won't let me have the hotel people throw him out . . . she seems to be afraid of him.' She paused and looked at the old man doubtfully. 'He makes life unbearable, and poor Grace gets more and more nervy. I felt something must be done.'

'I see,' said W.T. gently. 'But that doesn't answer my question, does it? How did you know where Jerry was to be found?'

'Oh, Lacy told us – at least, he told Grace. I wondered why you hadn't told us you were coming here when we were in Paris.'

'Lacy told your sister, did he? Do you know what else he told her?'

'No, she wouldn't tell me.' The girl frowned as she spoke. 'It's something that is worrying her. I can't think what it was. You see, Mr Challoner, ever since Lacy came the first time she's been so queer – so sort of reserved and shut away. I can't get anything out of her, and Lacy came so often and made himself so objection-able that I thought I must do something to get rid of him. I couldn't throw him out myself, so I was driven to coming to Jerry.'

'Yes?' said W.T.

Norah looked at him. 'So I came,' she said simply, 'and told him, and he just dashed out of the hotel shouting to me to wait for him.'

The detective nodded.

'Did you tell Jerry just exactly what you have told me?'

'Yes.'

'What did you ask him to do in the matter?'

The girl looked at him, surprised at his stupidity.

'There wasn't any need to ask,' she said. 'I just explained that the man was making himself a nuisance to us ...'

'And Jerry dashed off to knock his head off, I suppose?' said W.T. gravely.

'I suppose so,' said she, equally gravely, and added with a sudden return of her old anxiety, 'But he hasn't come back.'

W.T. rose to his feet.

'I'll go down and see what's going on,' he said.

'Will you? Shall I come with you?'

'No, I don't think so.' The old man shook his head as he spoke. 'You wait here for us. Jerry's all right,' he added more kindly. 'Don't worry. He's had worse people to deal with than Lacy in his time. We shan't be long.'

'Silly young fool!' said the detective testily to himself as he trotted down the hotel steps to the street. 'Silly young fool – as if things weren't sufficiently involved already ... The secret between Mrs Christensen and Gale seems fairly obvious, though ... He may have actual proof against her. Well, we shall see – we shall see.'

He strode on down the street, still grumbling to himself until he paused before the somewhat unprepossessing entrance to the hotel and café, the 'Maison Sud'.

It was an ordinary little place, not too clean or too airy, but a bright enough double-fronted affair with a striped canvas awning over the two windows, beneath which chairs and tables were set out on the pavement. At this hour of the day they were deserted, however. It was very hot, and the townsfolk preferred to remain within doors.

W.T. paused under the awning and mounted the single step that led into the café.

A brown-skinned waiter, with nothing remarkable about him save a magnificent moustache, shambled forward to inquire his pleasure.

W.T. asked for William Lacy, guessing that Gale would not use his own name anywhere if he could help it.

Yes, he was in; if Monsieur would follow the staircase he would find the door on the left-hand side. It had a number three upon it.

W.T. went up. The staircase was at the far end of the room, and as he came to the top of it he heard a sound that had not been audible in the café. It was an extraordinary noise, a sort of high-pitched howling, very thin and peculiarly suggestive to the listener. W.T. recognized it at once. It was a man swearing and crying with rage while someone held him by the throat.

The old man sprinted down the passage and kicked open the door of room No. 3.

The whining stopped as he entered, and a deep gasping breathing took its place. The room was in confusion. The bed, which took up the greater part of the floor space, had collapsed, the head and foot rails meeting together, forming a tent under which was a tousled mass of bedclothes, feathers and blood.

'Jerry,' said W.T. sharply.

'That you, Dad?' The boy's voice sounded cheerfully from the debris. 'This little swine got at me with a razor, so we had a dust-up. I've got him by the neck, but I've lost so much blood I haven't the strength to get out of this darned ironmongery. Give us a hand, will you?'

The detective came forward, and without exerting himself unduly, forced open the ironwork and extricated the two beneath.

Jerry was drenched in blood from a razor-slash that followed the line of his cheek-bone, but he was in good spirits and apparently very pleased with himself. Clarry Gale, on the other hand, was not so happy. He had had practically all the breath choked out of his body. As soon as he could breathe again he began to swear.

'Shut up!' said Jerry, turning on him.

W.T. looked at his son.

'What's the idea?' he said.

Jerry, who was staunching his face as best he could with a towel and cold water, spoke eagerly.

'I've got it, anyway,' he said.

'Got what?'

'Why, the thing this little swine here has been trying to sell to Mrs Christensen – some old love-letter, I think. Norah sent you on here, I suppose?'

W.T. nodded, and Jerry went on blithely:

'She came round to me,' he said. 'This little rat had been making her sister's life a hell. I guessed it was blackmail, so I came here. He was out, so I waited for him. When he came along I charged him with it, and he got offensive and accused me of coming here to get some letter or other for you without paying for it. That put me on to the scent at once, of course. I got hold of the letter, or whatever it is, and the little swab suddenly let out at me with the razor, and we finished up as you found us.'

'Oh,' said W.T. dryly. 'Where's the letter?'

Jerry produced a crumpled paper from his inside pocket and handed it to W.T. As it passed him, Clarry Gale dashed forward, snarling with impotent fury. Jerry hauled him back by the collar without speaking.

The detective unfolded the sheet of notepaper, and Jerry returned to the dressing of his wound.

For several minutes there was silence in the room save for the mutterings of Mr Gale, and eventually Jerry turned round.

'Well . . .' he began, and added as he caught sight of the detective's face, 'Hello – what's up?'

The old man was staring at the letter in his hand, his face flushed with astonishment.

'Well, that don't surprise you, do it?' said Mr Gale from his corner, some of his indignation vanishing before his interest in the situation. 'I've known that all along I have – that's been my theory from the very fust.'

'Here, what's all this about?' Jerry came forward, the towel still held up to his face. He crossed round behind the detective to read the letter over his shoulder; but the old man folded it hastily. Jerry stared at him.

'What's the idea?' he demanded.

Clarry Gale laughed.

'Go on, let 'im see it – 'e's sweet on 'er, ain't 'e? Do 'im good – teach 'im to keep 'is fice out of other people's business.'

Jerry glanced from Gale to his father, a sudden apprehension in his eyes.

'What was in that letter?' he said.

W.T. sighed and handed it back to him without a word.

Jerry read it through, and as he read his face changed.

Dear Mr Crowther [it ran.] Please leave me alone. I don't love you. I don't even like you, and I resent your attentions. I send back the shawl – naturally I can't take it. Please let this be final. Your continued efforts to make love to me on every possible occasion annoy me to the point of madness. If you don't leave me alone I shall do something really desperate – I warn you. You don't realize that you haven't a timid Victorian miss to deal with.

Nora Bayliss.

The date of the letter was September 2nd – three days before the murder.

'My God!' said Jerry weakly, and sat down on the one deal chair the room possessed.

Mr Gale began to laugh.

'That's wot you've bin fightin' for, me lad,' he said. 'That's slung you up proper, ain't it? ... Found out your precious lady-love ain't all she might be –' He got no further. W.T. made a dive to stop Jerry, but he was too late. The boy leapt from his chair, and a single blow sent Mr Gale to the floor where he lay weeping and threatening. Jerry sat down again.

'This is absurd, of course,' he said, holding out the letter – 'absurd as evidence, I mean. She must have written it in a temper, not realizing how it sounds.'

W.T. nodded.

'Of course,' he said. 'Of course; but this must be looked into, Jerry. If Gale was using this letter to blackmail Mrs Christensen it raises a very interesting question. Come here, Gale.'

The ex-burglar rose to his feet, grumbling and muttering to himself.

'Call this a noliday?' he said bitterly, standing there in the ruins of his bright blue suit, his face more pallid than ever and his unattractive, wispy hair standing on end on his narrow head. 'Call this a noliday?... Is this the way to treat a pore bloke wot's come to the Souf of France for 'is 'ealth? A proper picnic I've 'ad, ain't I? Ain't a man safe anywhere from the interference of the police?'

'That all depends on the man's habits,' said W.T. pleasantly. 'Now sit down – there's a piece of the bed over there that looks fairly safe – I want to talk to you.'

'I ain't goin' to say nothink,' said Mr Gale, in a tone that was partly sulky and partly defiant. 'You can't force me. You ain't got nothink agin' me, I shall prosercute that young feller for assault.'

'I shouldn't do that, Gale, and if I were you I should talk.' W.T. spoke quietly, but there was an underlying forcefulness in his tone that made the old lag glance up sharply.

'Wot yer mean?' he demanded suspiciously.

W.T. looked at him steadily.

'I am out here investigating a murder case, as you know, Gale,' he said, 'but that does not mean that I am blind to all other crimes that I may run into in the course of my inquiries. The penalty for blackmail is a heavy one, you know.'

'I don't foller anythink you're sayin',' said Mr Gale in the same semi-peevish tone.

W.T.'s eyes narrowed.

'Gale,' he said, 'you're going to talk – for your own sake as well as for anyone else's. Now out with it. Tell all you know about that letter.'

'I ain't goin' to . . . 'old 'ard, guv'nor. You ain't got no right to question me like this. I've gorn straight for ten years, I 'ave. You ain't got no right to force me to say nothink.'

'That ten years' honesty seems to have turned your head,' said W.T., not unpleasantly. 'It may be a miracle, but you shouldn't let it dazzle you. Where did you get that letter?'

'I found it.'

'Where?'

'Guv'nor, I ain't – '

'Where?' There was something in W.T.'s tone that brooked no argument, and Mr Gale weakened before it.

'In Crowther's desk.'

'After he was dead?'

'Yes.'

'You realized it might be valuable, and so you followed Mrs Christensen and Miss Bayliss out here to blackmail them?'

'Not so fast, guv'nor – not so fast – no putting of words into my mouth, *if* you please,' said the little man, some of his spirit returning.

W.T. shrugged.

'You may as well be honest now, Gale – it'll save a lot of time,' he said meaningly. 'You followed Mrs Christensen and Norah to Mentone simply because you thought there might be money in that letter. You may as well admit it.'

'Well,' said Mr Gale at last, 'I thought she might like to 'ave it, you know – wouldn't do to 'ave a letter like that lying about when the lawyers was clearin' up, now, would it?'

W.T. smiled contemptuously.

'And so you came all the way out here just to return that letter – that was nice of you, Gale.'

The little man shifted nervously.

'I knew the lady wouldn't see me out of pocket over it,' he murmured.

'Exactly,' said W.T. 'And you've called on her constantly these last two or three days to arrange about your expenses, I suppose?'

Clarry Gale nodded.

'Well, yes,' he said; 'in a way, yes.'

'And in a way, no,' snapped W.T. 'What were you doing with the letter here after you had seen her so often?'

'Why, guv'nor' – Mr Gale's expression was injured – 'you didn't expect me to part with the letter until we'd come to satisfactory terms?'

W.T. snorted.

'In other words, you were blackmailing her,' he said. 'That's a ten-year sentence nowadays, Gale.'

'Gawd! 'Ave a 'eart!' The old lag began to whimper again. 'I've been goin' straight for ten years, I have, and – '

'If I hear you mention that ten years again, Gale, I shall begin to suspect it,' said W.T. 'How about Mrs Phail in the Feering Park Crescent case?'

'Guv'nor!'

Clarry Gale's face was never an attractive sight, but at this moment it was ghastly. Always pallid, his flesh had now taken on a greenish tinge, and his little red-rimmed eyes goggled horribly. W.T. laughed shortly.

'We won't go into that,' he said. 'It's a long time ago, and the past may as well bury the past; but I don't think we'll stir up any trouble between us, do you, Gale?'

The man moved his dry lips with a curious clucking sound.

'All frien's 'ere,' he murmured huskily, all the sulkiness vanishing from his tone and subservience creeping into his manner.

'Well,' said W.T. sharply, 'how much has Mrs Christensen paid you already?'

'Three 'undred quid.'

'Three hundred pounds. And she hasn't had the letter. Good heavens, man, how did you do it?' ejaculated the detective.

Gale hesitated, but he was still trembling from the shock of the moment before.

'Well – you see,' he began breathily, 'she thought the girl done it.'

'What?'

Gale's little round eyes flickered and he shot a vindictive glance at Jerry.

'So do I,' he said. 'She went into the 'ouse just before 'im, didn't she? She *said* she was upstairs, but 'oo's to prove it? 'Er sister saw that at once.'

'When you pointed it out?' said W.T. swiftly.

Gale nodded. 'I may 'ave just mentioned it,' he said. 'Just to clinch an argument, like.'

'This is ridiculous,' cut in Jerry from the background. 'Both Gale and Mrs Christensen must be potty.'

'Love is blind,' said Mr Gale, and ducked. W.T. pressed his son back into his chair.

'It's no good hitting him,' he murmured. 'We've got to let him talk. Do you mean to say,' he went on slowly, returning to Gale, 'that Mrs Christensen actually believes that Miss Norah Bayliss killed Crowther?'

Gale nodded.

'Of course she does,' he said. 'That's why she forked out so 'andsome – money for nothink, it was – easy as kissin' your 'and.'

W.T. frowned. His theories were falling to pieces before his eyes.

'That first interview,' he said. 'Was she surprised? Did it come as a shock to her?'

'It knocked 'er all of a 'eap,' said Mr Gale. 'An' when she saw the letter ... Coo! I felt almos' sorry for 'er ... Of course, I worked it up proper before I showed the letter,' he added with a certain pride. 'Let 'er get all worked up wonderin' what I was drivin' at, and then shoved a copy of it at 'er sudden – mentioned you was in the town and told 'er wot was a-comin' to 'er sister. My word, she paid like a lamb after that. Money jus' chucked at me whenever I went near 'er.'

W.T. passed his long fingers through his white hair.

'Why,' he said at last – 'why did you go to Mrs Christensen and not to her sister? Surely Miss Bayliss would be the most likely to be interested in the letter?'

'I'm not barmy!' Mr Gale looked reproachfully at the detective. 'Mrs Christensen 'ad the money – interest wasn't no good to me without money. Besides, I didn't know if the girl 'ad done it – I thought she 'ad, but I didn't know. And she was the type to send me packin' if she was innercent by charnst, so I banked on the other sister – a little weak thing she is – not overmuch in the top storey, neither. I said to 'er, I said; "don't go discussin' this with your sister," I said; "don't even mention it, or she may get nerves and go confessin'," I said. So she promised she wouldn't say nothink.'

W.T. looked at him steadily, a hint of wonderment in his eyes.

'You are an old villain, aren't you, Gale?' he said at last. 'So crooked a touch of genius flashes out sometimes by accident.'

Mr Gale said nothing. He was not certain whether the detective's last remark was a reproach or a tribute, and was not anxious to go into it.

W.T. turned to Jerry.

'You go back to the hotel and get cleaned up, my boy,' he said. 'Don't let Norah see you if you can help it. I'll follow you.'

Jerry rose to his feet. He was very pale from loss of blood, and the razor-slash was hurting him.

'Right,' he said, and added suddenly, 'I say, Dad, you know that letter's all darn rot, don't you? I mean, you know there's nothing to it?'

'Of course I do.' W.T. spoke reassuringly, and as the door closed behind the boy he murmured to himself. 'It may be the truth – I don't know.' Then, the keen expression returning to his eyes, he looked again at Clarry Gale.

The little man was fidgeting nervously.

'Wot jer want to say ter me now?' he demanded. 'W'y've you sent 'im away? You said let the parst bury the parst, you said –'

W.T. nodded.

'I did,' he said, 'and so it shall.'

'You mean that?'

'I do.'

'Well, then – wot are we comin' to?' Mr Gale's tone was still apprehensive.

W.T. hesitated.

'A matter of curiosity,' he said. 'Did Crowther, alias Grant, *see* you – er – hit Mrs Phail?'

Gale nodded.

'Yus,' he said shortly. 'A naxident, it was,' he went on. 'She was jest goin' to screech, an' I let out at 'er. A pure naxident – an' 'e was watchin' – 'eard the row and crept down unbeknownst – watching like a cat watches a mahse.' He paused and licked his dry lips. 'An' never a word did 'e say. Gawd! Wot I went through! Never a word did 'e say, but as I stepped out of chokey five years later there 'e was waitin' for me, an' I never 'ad a moment's peace till the day 'e died.'

15 Where Were You?

W.T. walked back to his hotel, his hands clasped behind his back and his eyes bent upon the pavement.

Half an hour ago he would have sworn regretfully that Mrs Christensen had fired the shot, but now Gale's revelation had made all the difference.

Even supposing that the story was an entire fabrication – which, to say the least of it, was not likely – Mrs Christensen herself had dropped hints that she was not thinking of herself, which although he had not understood at the time now came back to the detective's mind very forcefully.

All things considered, therefore, the evidence against Mrs Christensen was practically cancelled out by this new evidence in her favour.

There remained – Norah.

Norah was, as Gale had said, not a weak type, but a high-spirited young woman who might possibly have committed the crime had she first convinced herself that she was acting in a good cause. Ridding the world of a monster, or some other silly rubbish, as the old man put it gloomily.

There was the letter. W.T. looked at it again. It was certainly a dangerous little document in the present situation, and as he re-read it he saw anew how likely Gale's story was – how easy it must have been to play upon the elder sister's nerves when he had such a note to back him up.

W.T. sighed. Norah must be interviewed at once.

When he entered the hotel lounge he found that the girl had disappeared. He made inquiries about her, but no one seemed to have noticed her departure, and presently he went up to Jerry's room to see how the boy was getting on. The first person he saw on opening the door was Norah, her sleeves rolled up to the elbows.

'I sent for a doctor,' she said. 'He's putting in some stitches, but it's not so bad as it looks.'

A bearded French doctor in shirt-sleeves was bending over Jerry, who lay back in a chair by the window.

W.T. sat down meekly and waited. Norah and the doctor bustled about, and the detective, remembering his own youth, reflected that Jerry was probably enjoying the situation.

The irony of the whole case irritated him. It was all so simple, so natural, and yet so involved and unsatisfactory. This romance of Jerry's with the girl was the last straw.

At last the doctor repacked his case, washed his hands, put on his coat, smiled, bowed, and departed. Norah cleared up the room and Jerry sat up and grinned as well as he could without hurting himself.

'I tried to sneak in the back way, but she spotted me from the window, Dad,' he said, not without a certain satisfaction. 'I couldn't get away from her.'

'I don't know where you'd be if it wasn't for me,' she said. 'You can't tie up a slash like that and hope for the best – you must have it sewn up at once or it shows for ever. I wouldn't listen to him,' she added, turning to the detective. 'I just sent for the doctor.'

W.T. smiled, but the expression in his eyes was uneasy. The crumpled letter in his pocket worried him.

'Miss Bayliss,' he said, 'I want to talk to you.'

'Yes?' There was nothing more than polite inquiry in the girl's tone, and the detective looked at her narrowly. She was smiling at him, her blue eyes wide with interest.

Jerry was not so carefree, however. He sat forward and spoke hastily.

'I say, Dad, you're not going into that letter, are you? Can't you see how perfectly absurd it all is? I mean – '

'My boy, I must go into everything,' said W.T. mildly. 'If there is nothing in it, it won't be unusual,' he added dryly.

'But I say, you can't!' the boy expostulated weakly. 'You can't
– I mean, that letter . . .'

'Jerry, if you talk so much you'll break those stitches.' Norah
smiled at him as she spoke, and then turned again to the detective.

'What is this about a letter?' she said. 'Anything *I* can tell
you?' Her tone was so frank and her smile so natural that W.T.
felt his suspicions fading.

He drew the letter out of his pocket and handed it to her.

She took it, surprised at first to see her own handwriting; but
as her eyes travelled down the page the colour rose in her face,
and her hand trembled.

'Did you write that?' There was a directness in the question
that could not be ignored.

The girl's nerve seemed suddenly to go to pieces. She stood
there scarlet-faced and stammering.

'No – yes – I don't know.'

'Dad, this is absurd!' cut in Jerry violently; but the old man
silenced him and, rising to his feet, placed a chair for the girl.

'Sit down,' he said gently, 'and then answer my questions. It
is very important.'

The girl took the chair thankfully and sank into it, and the
detective sat down opposite her, while Jerry leant forward peering
through his bandages, half angry, half apprehensive.

'Did you write that?' the detective repeated, indicating the
letter.

The girl nodded.

'Yes,' she said, and there was a hint of defiance in her tone.
W.T. frowned.

'Why did you write it?'

'Why are you questioning me like this? Surely you can't think
that I . . . ?' The girl's voice had grown unsteady in her nervous-
ness, and now she broke down completely and sat staring at him,
her breath drawing painfully and the colour coming and going
in her face.

'My dear child, I must question you.' W.T. spoke sharply. 'Do
you know that your sister has paid Gale – that is, Lacy – three
hundred pounds because of that letter?'

'Grace paid three hundred pounds?' The girl repeated his words in amazement. 'Three hundred pounds because of my letter? Why?'

'Because,' said W.T. slowly, 'he suggested, and she believed, that Eric Crowther's mysterious death and that letter might have some connection.'

'Mr Challoner, you must be mad.'

W.T. was disarmed. When he had hinted at his meaning she had appeared to be terrified, but now that he actually voiced it she immediately became calm, almost relieved. He returned to the letter, the only concrete fact he had to work upon.

'I'm afraid I must ask you to explain this, nevertheless,' he said, tapping it gently with his forefinger. 'You see,' he added, as the old child-like defiance crept into her eyes, 'in a mystery no clue must be disregarded.'

The girl nodded.

'I see,' she said, and stiffened as if for an ordeal. W.T. adopted his most fatherly manner.

'Now,' he said, 'this letter seems to suggest that Crowther was making himself a nuisance to you – irritating you with his attentions. Was that so?'

The girl nodded.

'Yes,' she said finally, and shot a half-doubtful, half-imploring glance at Jerry.

W.T. began to divine some of the reason for her reticence, and glanced at his son.

'Jerry,' he said, 'go and lie down in my room. I want to talk to Miss Bayliss alone.'

'I'll stay here,' said Jerry.

The girl looked at the detective pleadingly. 'Please let him stay,' she said.

W.T. shrugged his shoulders.

'Very well,' he said. 'But I warn you I want to hear all there is to say about this letter and the circumstances which led to its being written.'

Norah bowed her head in acquiescence, and he continued:

'In my first interview with your sister on the day of the tragedy she told me that she was being worried by Crowther. Was that true too?'

Norah hesitated.

'Ye–es,' she said at last, somewhat doubtfully.

'What does that mean?' said W.T. 'Was she – or was she not?'

Still the girl hesitated.

'She – she was, but not quite in the same way,' she said at last.

W.T. nodded understandingly.

'You mean that Crowther knew something – something that your sister was very anxious to keep a secret – and held it over her head?' he said.

The girl gasped.

'You – you know that?' she murmured.

W.T. saw that he had made a mistake, and turned back on his tracks.

'You didn't mean that?' he said swiftly. 'There was something else – some other way in which he annoyed her? What was it?'

Norah looked at him awkwardly.

'He worried her because of me,' she said. 'He wanted her to use her influence with me.'

W.T. cleared his throat.

'I see,' he said shortly. 'And – er – pardon me, Miss Bayliss, but did Crowther offer you – marriage?'

'Not at first.'

'Later?'

'Yes.'

'And you refused?'

'Of course.'

'Now, after you had refused him, did he still bother you?'

'Oh yes.'

'And you wrote him that letter?'

The girl nodded.

'Yes. He sent me an embroidered Spanish shawl with a – a horrible letter. I burnt the letter and sent back the shawl with that note – I was furious when I wrote it.'

'That was four days before the murder?'

'Yes.'

'How do you know that?' The detective spoke swiftly.

Norah looked at him in surprise.

'Because I remember,' she said simply.

'I'm afraid I must ask you to explain.' W.T. spoke warningly.

The girl was silent for a moment.

'Mr Challoner,' she said at last, 'you spoke just now of a secret my sister was anxious to keep.'

'Yes?'

'Well ...' The girl hesitated and the old detective suddenly saw her predicament.

'I know,' he said gently. 'I know all about it – you can speak to me with perfect confidence.'

'About – about Joan?'

'About Joan,' said W.T.

Norah sighed.

'That makes all the difference in the world,' she said. 'Don't you see – I can talk to you now.'

W.T. thrust his fingers through his hair.

'Oh, you women, you women,' he said wearily. 'When will you realize what is important and what is not?'

Norah's blue eyes were reproachful.

'You couldn't expect me to give away a secret like that, could you?' she said.

'My dear child' – the old detective was as exasperated as he ever permitted himself to become – 'an elephant is large compared with a mouse, but it is ridiculously small compared with Mount Etna. That secret may have been immense six months ago, but now we are faced with a larger and much more terrible secret. Don't you realize what a murder means?'

Norah shrugged her shoulders, and W.T. knew that she had followed his argument but was still not convinced.

'Yes,' she said, 'I see. But it's much easier to talk now.'

W.T. sighed.

'Well,' he said, 'let us start from the letter. You wrote that letter because you were angry with Crowther. He had been forcing unwelcome attentions upon you and upon your sister, using his knowledge of her secret to influence her in his favour as far as you were concerned.'

'Yes,' said Norah. 'But I didn't know he used the secret to influence her – I didn't know – about Joan then, you see.'

'You didn't know about the child?' W.T. was surprised. 'When did you learn about it?'

'On the day before the murder.'

'Who told you?'

'He did.'

'Who?'

'Crowther.'

'Crowther told you?' The old detective raised his eyebrows.

'Suppose you tell me about it,' he suggested.

The girl nodded.

'Very well. It was like this. After I wrote that letter he came over to see me, and I refused to see him; but he saw Grace, and afterwards I could see that she was very worried. I used to wonder why she put up with him. She used to say he was just trying to make love to her, and I believed it.'

'And all the time it was this affair of the child?' commented W.T.

'Yes ... I didn't know that then, though. All the next day I didn't see him, but on the third day – the day before he died, Crowther waylaid me in the garden and forced me to listen to him.' She paused, and looked at Jerry; but there was nothing but sympathy in the boy's face, and she continued:

'He began as usual trying to make love to me; and then suddenly, as I wouldn't listen, he caught my wrist and said he'd make me give in to him. Then he told me about – Grace and Joan – and said that if I didn't marry him he'd tell Roger, and – and everyone ...' Her young voice died away into silence.

'What did you say?'

'I laughed,' she said. 'Naturally. I didn't believe him.'

'Naturally,' agreed the old detective. 'Did he convince you?'

'Not – not quite. He was very plausible, though, and I began to be afraid. He told me to go into the office of our local newspaper and look up the files for December 1914. He said I'd find a notice of Jack Grey's death, with the date on which he left England in it, and that there'd be a photograph of him too, and I could see how like Joan was to him.'

'And the next day you went?'

She bowed her head.

'Yes,' she said softly; 'and it was true.'

'I met you coming back?' said Jerry.

'Yes,' she smiled at him. 'I didn't want you to bring my basket down to the porch in case he saw you – you see, I knew he was coming over.'

'Oh – how was that?' W.T. asked the question quickly.

The girl looked at him in surprise.

'He had written to Grace asking her to go over there,' she said. 'He did from time to time – just to be offensive, I suppose, and to try to make Roger jealous. She had told me she should take no notice of it, so I guessed he'd come over . . . he would be anxious to see me, too.'

W.T. looked at her.

Was it possible, he reflected, that she did not see where these admissions were taking her?

'Norah,' he said suddenly, 'what did you do when you got in: what was your first thought?'

The girl smiled.

'The blister on my heel,' she said. 'That's why I was so thankful to Jerry for bringing me home from the bus. I hobbled straight upstairs to take off my shoe and stocking – '

'Were you alone in your room when you heard the shot?' . . . W.T. put the question slowly. 'You said you were, you know, at the inquest.'

Norah nodded.

'I know,' she said. 'That was perjury or contempt of court or something awful like that, wasn't it?'

'Why – Norah, what are you saying?' Jerry's voice was husky with emotion. 'Where were you?'

'In the spare room,' said the girl, 'talking to Estah.'

'Talking to Estah? . . . Why didn't you say so before when asked at the inquest?' W.T. spoke sharply.

Norah looked at him helplessly.

'Don't you see,' she said, 'I wanted to make sure about Joan – I knew Estah would know, so I went to her at once. She had begun to tell me when we heard the shot. As soon as we realized there was going to be an inquiry we agreed to forget the conversation in case we were asked about it. I was to have remained in my room.'

W.T. bowed his head over his hands and ruffled his hair until it stood up all over his head like a snow-covered furze-bush.

'You were with Estah,' he repeated slowly to himself, as if he were dinning the words into his brain. 'You were with Estah . . . Then who in the name of all that's wonderful . . . ?' He paused and looked up sharply.

'I shall have to verify that, of course,' he said.

Norah nodded.

'If you can get Estah to talk she'll tell you the same story,' she said, and added, turning, 'How's your face, Jerry?'

W.T. looked at her slender back in despair. She seemed to have forgotten all about the murder.

16   Daylight

In reply to your inquiry, an interview with Estah Phillips resulted in a corroboration of Miss Bayliss's account. Great care was taken to ensure that there was no connivance between the two women, and there can be no doubt that they were together when the shot was fired.

                                                                    O. H. Deadwood.

W.T. put down the letter which he had been reading aloud, and looked across the hotel bedroom at Jerry.

'And that is that,' he said dryly.

'Well, naturally, what did you expect?' Jerry spoke contemptuously.

'I'll get to the bottom of this mystery if it's the last thing I do. Hang it all, Jerry, it happened – someone must have done it.'

Jerry shrugged his shoulders.

'Taking the fellow's temperament and habits into consideration, I should call it an act of God and leave it at that,' he said.

W.T. shook his head.

'I won't be beaten,' he said. 'Everything that happens in this world has a natural, simple, logical explanation. I'm not a believer in magic, Jerry. In this case there doesn't seem to be any proof except that everyone is innocent ... Everyone wanted to kill Crowther – everyone admitted they entertained the idea – everyone had an opportunity, and yet nobody did it. It's an incredible situation.'

Jerry looked at his father sharply.

'I say,' he said, 'you are convinced now that neither Mrs Christensen nor Norah know anything about it, aren't you?'

The old man nodded.

'Yes,' he said. 'I think I'm sure – as sure as anyone can be in this world.'

'Thank heaven for that,' said the boy. 'I'm glad you've got that letter. It'll make things so much more comfortable for the girls. I'll go down and tell Norah right away if you don't mind.'

'Very well,' W.T. spoke resignedly.

As the door closed behind the boy the man rose to his feet and walked slowly up and down the room.

'There must be some explanation,' he said aloud. 'Something simple – something so obvious that I've overlooked it – something – someone . . .' His mind went back to the beginning of the case, following it step by step through its tangle of secrets. Everything was there as he had said – motives, opportunities, inclination, and yet no proof against anyone, or even sufficient grounds for a strong suspicion.

He sat down wearily in his armchair by the window. His theories were in ruins about him, his weeks of work had taught him much, but led him no nearer to the vital points. The secret was as much a secret as it was on the day of the murder. He remained motionless for some time, thinking; then stretching out his hand, took an old battered book from the table at his side. It was *Gross's Criminal Psychology*, a book that he was in the habit of carrying about with him wherever he went.

He opened it at random, turning over the pages idly, his mind still half on the case that was worrying him. Suddenly his eye caught a phrase, and he stared at it. Then he laughed to himself as if at an absurdity, and went on reading. After a moment or so, however, his eye wandered back to the sentence that had arrested him, and again he stared at it, incredulity fighting with doubt in his mind.

At last he put the book face downward on the table and drew towards him his brownish-red notebook that looked so much like a Boy Scout's diary.

'Impossible,' he murmured. 'And yet . . .'

He took out a pencil and wrote a list of names down the page – the name of everybody in the house at the time of the murder, and one who was not.

For some time he sat staring at it, his forehead screwed up and his eyes narrowed. Then he sprang to his feet.

'My God!' he said. 'My God! Of course!'

Hastily he crammed things into a suitcase, and seating himself at the table scrawled a few words to Jerry.

On the track at last [he wrote]. Going to London. Wait till you hear from me. All the best.

                                                         Dad.

He folded the paper and slipped it into an envelope, leaving it with the concierge as he passed through the hall.

'No, no letters.' Jerry glanced down the rack and spoke with some disappointment. Norah looked up at him sympathetically. They had been dining together and had walked back to the hotel to see if the evening's post had brought any news from W.T. It was three days now since he had gone.

They wandered into the deserted and stuffy gilt-and-stucco drawing-room, and went out on to the balcony, where they stood for some time in silence.

The Riviera at night has a peculiar beauty of its own that is not quite equalled anywhere else.

The lights of the town winked and danced in the clear air with a gaiety of their own, and beyond, glittering in the moonlight, lay the Mediterranean, that blue jewel that seems to retain a little of its colour even in the darkness.

They were alone and the girl spoke softly.

'It seems an awful long time ago,' she said.

The boy replied without looking at her.

'Ages. It was horrible, of course; it must have been a nightmare to you – the whole business, I mean.'

She nodded.

'It has been – beastly,' she said. 'But not really worse than it was before – when he was alive.' She paused, and then went on again, her voice quiet and pleasant in the general dreaminess of the atmosphere. 'How queerly things happen!' she said. 'I mean you giving me a lift from the bus and then running right into it all, like that. You might so easily have come along ten minutes earlier or ten minutes later.'

The boy did not answer. He was staring out across the town to the sea. Somewhere hidden in the blackness he knew there were great mountains falling up against the sky, a world of incredible loveliness hidden under the coverlet of the dark. He felt rather like that about himself. His mind was in the dark. There was a screen between him and something, something utterly beautiful, and tonight, very near.

Instinctively he changed the conversation because he was afraid.

'Your sister,' he said – 'you're sure she's all right now?'

'Oh yes.' The girl spoke confidently. 'She's getting to be her old self again – now that she's sure her secret is safe. It has been terrible for her, poor dear ... she loves Roger, you see. It must have been ghastly for her to know that at any moment he might hear about Joan – he worships that kid. It would break her heart.'

Jerry nodded.

'What will they do?' he said. 'Stay at the White Cottage?'

'Oh no; we shall go abroad, I think. Roger has been talking of it for years. He came from the Argentine, you know, and I expect we shall all go out there. I know Grace wants to get right away from England – she's been so unhappy there, you know. I think that's what will happen.'

Jerry glanced at her. Her face was very pale in the faint light, and the clear-cut profile against the shadow of the sky was very lovely. He sighed.

'The Argentine?'

'Yes – all Roger's people are over there.'

Jerry was silent.

'You'll go too?'

'Oh yes!'

Her hand lay on the iron rail of the balcony. Jerry could see it very white in the darkness. He put his own over it.

'I love you, you know,' he said simply.

She did not speak for a moment, but stood very straight, staring out across the town. Then she chuckled a little with sheer happiness.

'Yes, I know,' she said.

'And you?' He put the question fearfully.

'I love you,' she said, without hesitancy.

'Shall we get married?'

She turned to him, and there was that expression in her eyes that is half adoration and half triumph.

'Shall we?' she said.

Jerry pulled her towards him and kissed her lips.

'*I* think so,' he said, and there was silence between them for a long time after that.

By and by she stirred at his side.

'Jerry,' she said, 'what will happen about this case – will your father give it up?'

The boy shook his head and his arm tightened about her shoulders.

'No,' he said, 'I'm afraid not. He'll go on to the bitter end.' He paused and looked down at her. 'But whatever happens,' he went on, 'we'll stick together, don't you think so?'

The girl laid her head on his shoulder and sighed contentedly.

'I do, my dear,' she said. 'Oh, Jerry, I am glad of you!'

The boy laughed and kissed her. A step in the room behind them made them start and the next moment the concierge appeared at the window.

'A cablegram for monsieur,' he said.

Jerry took the flimsy envelope and tore it open. The next moment an incredulous expression appeared on his face.

'Thank you,' he said briefly to the man, and, as he disappeared, handed the wire to Norah.

She took it and read it in the faint light from the drawing-room windows.

Abandoning case finally [it ran]. Shall be at home if you want me.

Dad.

The girl stared at it and then glanced up at the boy.

'I don't quite understand,' she said. 'Does that mean he can't find out who did it?'

Jerry looked at her gravely, an anxious expression on his face.

'No,' he said slowly, his voice oddly husky and afraid. 'It means ... he has.'

17 The End of the Story

It was one of those pleasant, lazy days in summer when the over-bushy tree-tops stir themselves heavily like fat oxen in the sun, and the shadow under the elms at the far end of Jerry's garden was very comfortable.

They were having tea out there. the three of them – Jerry, his wife, and W.T., who looked not a day older than he had done on that evening seven years ago when he had left Mentone in such excitement.

Jerry looked a little older perhaps but life had been kind to him. Norah was radiant. Marriage and two babies had given her a new interest without robbing her of her beauty. Altogether they were a happy tea-party, and laughter mingled with the tinkle of china.

The White Cottage Mystery was a tabooed subject in the household. From the time of his cablegram to the present moment, W.T. had obdurately refused to discuss it, and his children, after several unsuccessful attempts to draw the truth from him, had respected his wishes and allowed him to keep his secret.

The Christensens had sailed to the Argentine almost directly after Norah's marriage. The White Cottage had been sold to a retired grocer who had distempered it buff colour and re-christened it 'Acacia Cot'. The whole affair was forgotten by the public, who had mercifully never been greatly interested.

On this particular afternoon, however, a remark of Norah's had brought an echo of the whole mysterious business.

'Oh,' she had said, 'of course, Joan is coming to tea. She sails on Friday.'

W.T. looked up. 'I haven't seen her since – since – that affair,' he said. 'Let me see, she's twelve and a bit now, isn't she?'

Norah nodded.

'Yes, and looks sixteen,' she said. 'An extraordinary child – just the same as she was as a kid – just as reticent and sort of "fey".'

The old detective set his teacup down on the table before he spoke.

'She doesn't like England, I understand,' he said. 'Going back again after only one term at school?'

'Yes. Isn't it absurd?' Norah laughed as she spoke. 'I wrote Grace and told her that we'd look after the child in the holidays, but Joan wants to go back – she says she hates being at school.'

'She's an odd sort of kid,' put in Jerry. 'Not the type to get on well at school – a wild creature, very frank and unexpected.'

'Hush!' said Norah. 'She's coming down the path. Don't let her think you're talking about her.'

The conversation was duly changed, and Jerry and his father were discussing the condition of the lawn by the time the young lady in question came up.

W.T. looked at her with interest.

She was a tall, sturdy youngster, heavy-boned and strong, with big black eyes and long pig-tails. She walked with a stride, her little frill of skirt fluttering about her long legs, absurd and inadequate, a polite gesture to convention only.

The detective could see what Jerry had meant when he said that she was not the type to get on well at school.

She was obviously a creature who required freedom. A young savage almost. There was no self-consciousness in her bearing. She smiled frankly round the table and sat down.

'Oh,' she said, looking at W.T. as Jerry introduced him, 'I've heard of you from Mother.'

'I remember *you*,' said the detective. 'Have you forgotten me?'

The child looked at him doubtfully.

'I don't remember you,' she said. 'Was I very young?'

'You were – rather. They tell me you're going to leave us. You've only just come.'

She nodded and laughed.

'I know. I can't stand it at school – I don't fit in over here. Miss Garnham says I'm not civilized.'

'You like it better over there?'

'Rather!' There was no mistaking the enthusiasm in her young voice. 'It's – *big* over there,' she said; 'big enough to move about and stretch yourself – d'you know?'

W.T. laughed and nodded.

'Yes,' he said, 'I know.'

The girl turned to Norah.

'How are your children, Auntie?' she inquired.

'All right,' said Norah, and added after a frown and a pause, 'except for one thing. Do you know, I think your long association with crime, Dad, is – is coming out in Bill.'

'My dear!' expostulated Jerry.

W.T. laughed. 'This sounds serious,' he said. 'What signs of depravity has young four-year-old been showing?'

'Well,' said Norah, 'I hardly like to say it, but he – *steals!*'

'How horrible!' said W.T. 'I'll get a warrant.'

Norah grimaced at him.

'Don't tease me,' she said. 'I'm really quite worried about it. He stole a whole bladder of lard off one of those tray things outside a pork-butcher's when I left him there in the pram – and hid it under the coverlet. I didn't find it till I got home ... I felt so terribly awkward going back to pay for it.'

'Oh, my dear girl, you are an old silly.' Jerry put his arm round his wife as she spoke and hugged her.

Norah raised her eyebrows.

'I don't know what you're all laughing at,' she said. 'I thought it was awful. Fancy going into a shop and saying, "Please can I pay for that bladder of lard you've lost? My baby stole it."'

'My dear child,' W.T. spoke mildly, 'if I may mention it, Bill's crime seems only to horrify you so much because of the awkwardness it caused you.'

'Not at all,' said Norah. 'I was thinking entirely of my son's moral nature. A baby who would steal a bladder of lard would steal anything.'

'Rather,' said Jerry. 'The kid's a fool. That's all there is in that.'

'I don't think so,' said Norah. 'I think it shows a definite criminal tendency. When I said, "Did you take that, Bill?" he beamed at me, and said, "No." . . . So I spanked him, of course.'

'Poor old Bill,' said Jerry, whose sympathies were with his son entirely.

'I'm quite worried about it,' Norah persisted. 'Wouldn't it be awful if he grew up in the habit of stealing.'

W.T. opened his mouth to reply, but Joan, who had listened to the conversation unsmilingly, forestalled him.

'I shouldn't worry, Aunt,' she said. 'I think you do things without realizing that they're wrong or dangerous when you're a child. I remember firing a gun at a man once.'

W.T. put out his hand to lay it on her arm, but Jerry's expression prevented him. Both the boy and his wife had turned to the child, their eyes wide and inquiring, the laughter dying suddenly out of their faces.

Joan continued, quite unconscious of the effect she was producing, while W.T. leant back in his chair, his eyes closed and his face immovable.

'Of course, I don't remember it very well,' the child went on. 'I think it must have been when we first went out to the Argentine . . . I only remember the man's face. He was very big and fat and red, with little monkey eyes.' She paused and laughed. 'Have I shocked you all?' she said. 'Don't worry – I don't think I hurt the man.'

Norah drew a sharp breath. Her face was very pale.

'Tell us about it, dear,' she said, striving to keep her voice steady. The child looked at her curiously, but was nothing loth to talk, and went on with her reminiscences light-heartedly.

'I don't remember anything about it really,' she said, 'except that I did it. I know I hated the man – I used to call him Satan to myself. Old Estah said he was Satan. Do you remember Estah, Aunt?'

Norah nodded. She was white to the lips, and Jerry, who was none too steady himself, put his hand over hers.

W.T. alone was apparently unmoved by the story. He sat quiet, his eyes shut.

'Estah hated this man,' Joan continued. 'She used to tell me how wicked he was until I was terrified of him. He used to make trouble. I remember people were always cross when he was about.'

'Yes?' said Jerry, unable to keep silent any longer. 'And so you shot him?'

Joan laughed.

'Uncle Jerry, that sounds dreadful!' she said. 'I don't really remember what had happened, but I know I hated Satan, and one day I was in the garden with a pail in my hand. I don't remember where it was or what I was doing – it's rather like a dream now – but I know I passed a door, and looked in and saw Satan leaning over a table laughing at me. I was just scared of him, and I hated him, and I suddenly remembered that there was a gun in the corner of the room . . .' She paused and looked round her. 'It sounds shocking, doesn't it,' she said, and laughed again. 'Estah had told me about the gun. She said to me, "Don't touch that; it might go off and hurt somebody." And so when I saw Satan there I remembered the gun, and I remembered thinking that he ought to be hurt if he was so wicked.'

Jerry's hand closed tightly over his wife's, and she trembled beside him.

'I lifted the gun,' the child went on; 'it was terribly heavy; I could hardly carry it. Satan just laughed at me, and that made me cross, so I banged it down on the table at him and I squeezed the trigger part with all my strength. There was an awful bang, and I shut my eyes and ran out into the garden and picked up my pail . . . I don't remember any more. But I'm sure that happened.'

There was utter silence for some seconds after she had spoken, and presently her gurgling chuckle echoed again.

'It sounds awful, I know,' she said, 'but I'm sure it did him good. I never remember hearing of him again, anyway. I scared him, I suppose. I know I felt I must be very quiet about it in case Estah was cross with me for touching the gun. So Bill's no worse than I was, Aunt.'

Norah took out her handkerchief and hid her face in it, and W.T. spoke, forcing a jocular note into his voice.

'Joan,' he said, 'that's a very shocking story. I am appalled by it. When I think I am having tea with a young woman as wicked as all that it horrifies me and makes my hair go white.'

'It's white already,' said Joan, laughing at him.

He drew her towards him and perched her on his knee.

'That shows how clever I am,' he said, 'and how unutterably old and respectable; and so you mark well what I say. Don't you go telling fairy-stories like that to everyone you meet.'

The girl blushed.

'That's not a fairy-story,' she said. 'I did ...'

'No,' said the old detective very firmly. 'Don't believe it. That's a dream. Haven't you ever dreamt something so clearly that you thought in the morning that it was true? I dreamt I was an ancient Briton once. I was so convinced about it that I nearly came down to breakfast in a skin rug – that's what happened to you.'

'I don't think so,' the child said doubtfully. 'I do remember Satan, and – '

'Of course you do,' said W.T. 'And don't I remember the coracle I sailed in, and my dog that was as big and as fierce as a lion? Of course I do, but it didn't happen; it wasn't true. Honestly Joan, wasn't it a dream?'

The child hesitated.

'It was an awful long time ago,' she said at last. 'It might have been a dream ...'

'Of course it was,' said W.T. 'Of course it was; and a bad dream, too. You can do better than that ... When are you going back to school?'

'Now,' said the child, grimacing at him. 'I've got to get in to prep., but I'm not worrying – in a week's time I'll be free for ever and ever and ever.'

W.T. released her.

'Good-bye, then, my dear,' he said. 'Put that cake of Norah's in your satchel – perhaps with care you could eat it in prep. – and, Joan ...'

'Yes?'

'Never tell your dreams.'

'All right. Good-bye, Aunt Norah. Good-bye, Uncle Jerry.' She took the cake and ran off, a wild colt of a creature – all legs and arms.

As soon as she was out of earshot, Jerry looked at his father.

'Dad – you – you *knew*,' he said huskily.

The old man nodded.

'Yes,' he said slowly. 'There's the truth of the White Cottage Mystery ... Estah Phillips was the murderess of Eric Crowther, although she never knew it.'

Norah began to cry softly, and Jerry put his arm round her.

'Hush,' he said. 'It's nothing to worry about ... It can't be helped. It's one of those queer terrible judgements that do happen from time to time. Don't cry, old lady.'

Norah sat up, and wiping her eyes, hastily turned to the old man. 'How did you find out?' she demanded.

W.T. hesitated.

'I made a vow never to breathe a word about that murder,' he said at last, 'but now you know so much you may as well hear it all. It was Gross who first gave me the hint. I was in despair, as you know – everyone ought to have done it, but by the evidence nobody had. I took down *Gross's Criminal Psychology* and opened it at random, and almost the first words I read were something like this:

The child has its own views as to what a person's deserts are. These views can rarely be judged by our own.

He paused and stared in front of him, recalling the scene to his mind.

'Of course,' he went on at last, 'I didn't pay much attention to them at first, but somehow they took hold of my mind. I began to think of the child, and of that queer old woman Estah, who was just the type to bring up a kid with a hatred of Crowther. After all, I argued, a child only knows what it is told. The difference between God and the Devil is only clear to it because it has been *told* that God is good and Satan is bad.'

Again he was silent but neither of his listeners spoke, and by and by he went on.

'Estah had been pretty frank with me – more than likely she talked a great deal to the child . . . The way the murder was committed suggested that it was unpremeditated, but not accidental – whoever had killed Crowther meant to kill him at the moment but had not thought it out beforehand. Again, the child was the only person round that side of the house, and the child was the only person who, probably not realizing what she had done, would not have the crime on her conscience and so become nervy. The more I thought of it the more it struck me as being true. For a moment I thought that she was too small to lift the gun, but again when I reflected I realized that she was not. The way the gun was fired from the table fitted in with the theory, too. It seemed to grow more and more likely every time I thought of it.'

'And so you went to Estah?' said Jerry.

W.T. nodded.

'I did,' he said; 'but not until I had remembered one thing – Cellini's story of the flicker of white round the window-post. Mrs Christensen, I knew, had worn a tweed costume in the garden. Norah had on a blue frock, and Estah was in black. And women don't wear white frilly petticoats nowadays, I understand. The only likely person to be in white was the baby – her skirts, too, would be full enough to swing out a little behind her. As soon as I had this clear in my mind I went to Estah. She admitted she had talked to the child about Crowther, and told me that the baby called him Satan.'

He paused and sighed.

'I asked her for the frock that the child had worn on the day of the murder, and as soon as she brought it out I knew I was on the right track. It was a very frilly, white affair with an enormously wide skirt.'

'And that convinced you?' said Norah.

W.T. shook his head.

'Not quite. I took it to Cellini. He recognized it.'

His voice died away into silence, and Jerry spoke.

'Then you decided to throw up the case?'

The old detective nodded.

'Yes,' he said. 'Estah was guilty of the thought, but the child was the actual firer of the shot.'

'So you risked your reputation,' said Norah, 'and put up with all that rubbish from Deadwood and Co. – '

W.T. smiled.

'My dear,' he said, 'my reputation had at most only another few years to run. Hers has to stand a lifetime.'

There was silence after he had spoken. Suddenly Norah rose to her feet. Jerry looked up at her. 'Where are you off to, dear?'

The woman glanced over her shoulder; she was already half-way across the lawn.

'I'm going to the nursery,' she said. 'I want to tell my Bill how – how *good* everybody is, and get it well into his mind.'

More Crime and Mystery in Penguin Omnibus Editions

THE MARGERY ALLINGHAM OMNIBUS

Whether he's faced with a deadly game of hide-and-seek in a remote Suffolk house, protecting a retired judge from assassination or an international ring of rather special art collectors, Albert Campion holds his own. His deceptively innocent appearance and mild manners mislead not a few in the three novels contained here: *The Crime at Black Dudley*, *Mystery Mile* and *Look to the Lady*.

'Always of the elect, Margery Allingham now towers above them' – *Observer*

THE NICOLAS FREELING OMNIBUS

Because of the Cats, *Gun Before Butter* and *Double-Barrel* – three gripping, high-tension thrillers are included here, and they all feature that most unorthodox detective, Van der Valk. Whether he is asked to investigate an unpleasant case of teenage violence, sent to solve a commonplace murder, or assigned to a dreary town to uncover the author of poison-pen letters, he always gets the cases no one else wants. Cool, amiable and incurably curious, he probes the routine surfaces . . . and finds himself in dangerous places.

'Van der Valk remains the most subtle, complex and interesting of fictional police detectives' – Edmund Crispin in the *Sunday Times*

THE MICHAEL INNES OMNIBUS

Clues baffle and suspects abound in these exhilarating novels: *Death at the President's Lodging*, *Hamlet, Revenge!* and *The Daffodil Affair*. In them the literary touch of Inspector Appleby is called upon to tackle the macabre murder of a University President, the shooting of the Lord Chancellor while he was acting the part of Polonius, and the simultaneous disappearance of a half-witted girl from London and a half-witted horse from Harrogate.

'A master – he constructs a plot that twists and turns like an electric eel: it gives you shock upon shock and you cannot let go' – *The Times Literary Supplement*

THE BLACK HOUSE
Patricia Highsmith

Brilliant ... disturbing ... menacing ... these eleven sinister stories reveal Patricia Highsmith's characters breaking the social laws (often unconsciously) and paying the price. They are victims trying to behave like protagonists – and the results are often fatal.

'Nothing is certain when we have crossed *this* frontier. It is not the world as we once believed we knew it, but it is frighteningly more real to us than the house next door' – Graham Greene

THE BLOOD OF AN ENGLISHMAN
James McClure

At first, it looked much like any other dead body – breathtaking in its own way, of course, but nothing special ... Then he saw that the arm bones had been fractured by a knot, a knot that must have been tightened by a giant – or a human gorilla.

The celebrated detective team of Lieutenant Kramer and Sergeant Zondi are on the track of what appears to be a gigantic killer possessed of hideous strength. A murderer so out of the ordinary should be easy enough to find, yet to Kramer's intense embarrassment, he proves remarkably elusive.

LANDSCAPE WITH DEAD DONS
Robert Robinson

The wit and iconoclasm that we expect from the presenter of BBC Radio's *Stop the Week* abound in this malicious little academic exercise ... For when the Vice-Chancellor is despatched among the statues with a dessert knife, the dreaming spires of Oxford are rudely awakened and all Hell is let loose. Caught with their trousers down (in front of the Ladies' Eight too!), the unlucky thirteen of Warlock College are given the third degree by Inspector Autumn of Scotland Yard, and all is revealed.